OSIRIS DIED IN AUTUMN

A CRIME CLUB SELECTION

"I wish there was a gentle way of doing this," the young police lieutenant said, "but there isn't. Dr. Gregg is dead. . . . He literally never knew what hit him."

In the silence of her mind, Natalie Keith shouted a denial. She had been in Will's arms only a few hours earlier. Now, as the realization of his death hardened into a profound, unutterable sense of loss, she reluctantly acceded to Lt. Jensen's request to assist the police in their hunt for her fiance's murderer. She had no choice; as the last known person on the University campus to see him alive, she was a suspect herself. But neither Natalie nor any of Dr. Gregg's other colleagues on the faculty could shed any light on his enigmatic past—a past which suddenly reached into the present with a violent threat to Natalie's life.

Scene: New York State

 CLASSIC PUZZLER

Lee Langley

OSIRIS DIED
IN AUTUMN

PUBLISHED FOR THE CRIME CLUB BY
DOUBLEDAY & COMPANY, INC.
GARDEN CITY, NEW YORK
1964

2041

All of the characters in this book are fictitious, and any resemblance to actual persons, living or dead, is purely coincidental.

Library of Congress Catalog Card Number 64–19173
Printed in the United States of America
First Edition

TO MY MOTHER,
with love and admiration

. . . But Iris, when she heard of it, cut off in that place a lock of her hair and put on a mourning weed. . . .

Plutarch's Tale of Osiris, paraphrased from the translation in *Never to Die,* by Mayer and Prideaux, New York: The Viking Press, 1938.

CHAPTER I

October is a whimsical month. At times a parody of summer, at others a gleeful overture to autumn and, beyond that, to winter; it is a time of harvests garnered in, of closed windows, and of fires on the hearth, a time of reflection and a time for the re-ordering of life.

It was unusually cold for the second night of October, and, as if impressed by the fact, both town and campus lay quiet. The empty streets seemed larger than life, and the few lighted windows overlooking them were beacons to the curious. The only centers of overt activity were the bars and the all-night movies. Otherwise the city sprawled in somnolent darkness while the University, which in daylight seemed more its wrestling partner than its third-largest industry, had wrapped itself in medieval still.

There were of course those of whom circumstances required wakefulness. Policemen, for instance. George Durwent, Ed.D., dean of arts and sciences, found himself in sleep-hazed telephone conversation with one of their number who was trying to explain that something had happened to a member of the faculty.

"No," the dean said, "I don't know who Will Gregg's doctor is. Allan Madison is the University's man."

"Thanks," the firm-voiced caller said pleasantly enough, "but we need his own physician. Can you give me the name of a close friend?"

"Well"—the dean scowled at his slippered feet—"I suppose Professor Keith—"

"His address, please?"

"Nine-twenty-one Stone Avenue, but—"

"Thank you." The policeman sounded grateful to have accomplished this much. "Call him, please, and say we're sending a car to pick him up in half an hour. We'll send one for you too."

"Me!" the dean objected, forgetting the thing he had been trying to say. "Me! Where?"

"At Doctor Gregg's house. I'll give you the details when you get here."

Durwent hung up and stood as if mesmerized. Between being half asleep and having a miserable cold, he found it hard to concentrate, let alone understand what was happening.

"George," his wife asked, coming out of the bedroom, "who was that?"

"The police," he answered. "Something's happened to Will."

"What has Natalie Keith to do with it?"

"Nothing," he answered, and sneezed loudly. "They wanted the name of a friend, and I thought of Natalie. I'd better call her."

Elaine Durwent frowned. "If this is serious the police won't want to involve a woman. Why not call Edward Ken?"

The dean made a wry face. "I don't like either of them," he said petulantly, "but of the two, I'd prefer Natalie."

"I doubt that your personal feelings will matter much," she said. "I'll go make some hot coffee."

Durwent nodded absently and picked up the phone. In the year since he had been made dean one thing after another seemed to have gone wrong. He almost wished he had taken that post as professor of education at the state teachers' college. At least there people would have understood him, and the money would have been the same. With a deep sigh, he began dialing Natalie Keith's number.

There had been frost during the second night of October, and Natalie Keith, wakened sometime between midnight and the dawn, recognized its signature on the windows of her bedroom. This was the first fact her mind grasped until the telephone rang again. It was, she noted, twelve-two A.M.

"It's awfully late," she announced without prologue, "or possibly awfully early. It depends on how you look at it. Who is this, anyhow?"

12

"George Durwent. Natalie, something odd seems to have happened at Will Gregg's place—"

Her hand tightened on the hard plastic of the receiver and she awoke with the suddenness of a bubble bursting. "Where is he?" she demanded.

"I don't know," Durwent answered. "The police just called—"

"*Police!*"

"Yes." The dean sneezed explosively. "I think they're at Will's place. Anyhow, they're sending a car for you in half an hour."

"George," she said with rigid calm, "will you kindly tell me what's happened? Has Will had an accident? Is he ill? Has there been a fire?"

"I don't know, Natalie," he said impatiently. "I'm just as confused as you are."

"I'm not confused, George, I'm upset. There *is* a difference."

"And the police will be there before you're even dressed. Please hurry, Natalie."

Irritated, she hung up without ceremony. She was waiting in front of her apartment house when the police car arrived. "I believe you're looking for me," she said, approaching it.

The young patrolman in the passenger's seat smiled disarmingly. "Not unless you're Professor Keith," he said.

"That's exactly who I am. Can you tell me what this is all about?"

A look of surprise and wariness crossed his face. He did not answer at once, but reached over and opened the back door. "Hop in," he said. "Pardon our shabby upholstery."

She climbed dutifully in. "Can you tell me what's happened?" she asked again as the car started up.

"I wish I could, ma'am," the patrolman said, turning to look at her over the back of the seat, "but all I know is we're to take you to two-thirty-seven University Boulevard."

"Has there been an accident," she prompted, "or a fire?"

"Gee, I'm sorry—"

"No, I am," she apologized. "I've no right to badger you. It's just—well, Doctor Gregg is an old friend, and I'm scared half out of my wits by all this."

"Sure you are," he said gently, "you've been hauled out of

13

bed in the middle of the night by a bunch of cops, and that's enough to scare anyone. I wish I could help."

He's humoring me, Natalie thought with detached recognition; he's treating me like some hysterical female— Well, by gum, that's exactly what I am! I've got to believe this is nothing serious.

"Can you tell me who's in charge of whatever's going on?" She tried to sound reasonable and even slightly amused.

"Chris Jensen," he answered. "He's a lieutenant of detectives, and one of the best."

"Jensen," Natalie mused, "Jensen—wasn't he the man who caught that ex-convict who shot the bank guard?"

"Well, yeah—but detectives work on all sorts of cases."

There he goes again, Natalie thought; humoring me. Either I'm borrowing trouble, or this is really serious.

"Two-thirty-seven University," the driver announced. "We're here."

She peered through the window and was aware of a sudden climax to her apprehensions. There were too many lights on in Will Gregg's house. "Fastest trip crosstown I've ever made," she said aloud. "Thank you both—"

"That's okay." The patrolman got out and opened the door for her. "Take it slow."

She mumbled something and started up the path toward the Victorian splendor of Will's house. The slate stones were uneven, and the puddles left by yesterday's rain were skimmed with ice. The walk had never been so long, and each step seemed to take her farther from reality: something had happened to Will, and she was torn between wanting to know what, and being afraid to find out.

George Durwent was waiting on the porch and came to the top of the steps to meet her. The porch light, dim in its yellowed octagon globe, made him look tired and sick. She wished suddenly that she had got there before him and been able to speak to the police in private.

"It's always good for a cold," she observed acidly, "to stand around outdoors at one o'clock in the morning."

"I just got here," he answered defensively. "Shall we go in?"

He led the way across the porch, and the old boards, resenting

14

their combined weight, creaked mournfully. He rang, and almost at once the door was opened by a uniformed policeman.

"Professor Keith?" he asked.

"No, I'm Dean Durwent. This is Professor Keith. I think we're expected—"

The policeman nodded, unperturbed by the needless comment. "I'll tell the lieutenant you're here. Getting colder out, isn't it?"

She had spent hundreds of hours in Will Gregg's living room in the past ten years, yet now Natalie found it strange and depressing. Abruptly, unaccountably, it had become just another display of slightly stuffy, slightly threadbare turn-of-the-century domesticity. It could be used, she decided, as a stage set for *Goodbye, Mr. Chips.*

"May I take your coat, Natalie?" Durwent asked.

She made a conscious effort to be civil. "No, thank you. It's chilly in here. Or maybe it's just me."

"I told Will last week to turn on his furnace," the dean said testily.

"He probably hasn't ordered his fuel oil yet." She smiled. "He always waits for first frost. Then, of course, he waits for delivery. I've often wondered why he pays a secretary. Admittedly, Renata Duval isn't exactly a gem of efficiency, but still—"

"Dean Durwent?" a deep male voice asked. "I'm Jensen."

The dean rose, offered his hand, and introduced Natalie. "I hope we weren't too long getting here," he apologized needlessly.

"On the contrary, your timing was perfect."

"You seem slightly disconcerted, Lieutenant," Natalie said. "Did we, perhaps, come *too* quickly?"

"No, of course not." Jensen went through the ritual of producing and offering cigarettes. "To be completely frank, what's disconcerting me is *you,* Professor. I don't know why, but I assumed you'd be a man."

"I apologize for my inadequacies, Lieutenant." She spoke rather more sharply than she intended. "But since I'm here, perhaps I can help. Can you tell us what's happened?"

Jensen lit her cigarette and his own, using the time to study the two before him. The dean, a tall man beginning to run to

15

fat, wore well-tailored tweeds that fit his body but somehow not his personality. Professor Keith, in a navy suit and a swept-back hair style, could have been the kind of highly skilled, literate actress whom one might mistake for a college professor. A woman so handsome in early middle age must surely, he decided, have been beautiful in youth.

"I'm sure you're both aware," he began, "that we've been having an epidemic of burglaries in this neighborhood." He paused and dropped the burned-out match carefully into an ashtray. "About eleven this evening the people across the road noticed Doctor Gregg's front door standing open, and called the precinct. A prowl car investigated, and called us."

"'Us' being exactly who or what?" Natalie asked.

Jensen look straight at her. "The Central Homicide squad."

The muscles between Natalie's ribs went rigid so that her chest ached and it was difficult to breathe. Over the pounding of her heart she heard herself ask why.

"I wish there was a gentle way of doing this," Jensen said, "but there isn't. Doctor Gregg is dead. It happened very quickly, and from what I can tell he literally never knew what hit him."

The hammer in her chest became a pile driver, and she struggled to breathe. In the silence of her own mind she shouted his name, half in fear and half in denial: he could not be dead—not Will! Not Will of the low, dark voice and the kindly eyes. She had left him only hours ago, and she could still feel the ghost of his embrace about her.

No, not dead. Not Will.

The closeness of so many years, the wonder of being together that even campus gossip could not spoil, could not end this way. They had waited so long and denied themselves so much— No, he was lying, this young stranger with the gun at his belt.

"Are you all right, Professor?" Jensen asked, alarmed by her sudden pallor and the glazed look of her eyes.

"I don't believe it." She was surprised that her voice sounded so much like itself.

"I'm sorry," he said gently, "I wish I could say this was some sort of macabre joke, but it isn't. Doctor Gregg was killed,

16

apparently by a burglar. His desk was ransacked, his wallet emptied, and an attempt made to jimmy a locked file. That's one reason why I wanted you and the dean here. I'll need to know what's missing from his art collection and get descriptions to the dealers immediately."

"That's Natalie's business." Durwent nodded toward her. "She's an archaeologist. You know Will's collection rather well, don't you, Natalie?"

Bastard, she thought, wielding the name like a mental bludgeon; small-souled, narrow-minded bastard! Know Will's collection? I helped plan it.

She was aware that Jensen was studying her with professional skill, and she knew she would have to answer him and do so in a way that would protect her relationship to Will.

"I'll be glad to help in any way I can, Lieutenant," she said, "and George is right, I do know the collection well. Doctor Gregg often asked my advice."

Jensen, apparently satisfied that she was trustworthy, nodded. "Thanks, we'll get to that in time. Right now, I need the answers to some more basic questions. The usual routine, you know."

He began then, asking them when they had last seen Will, what he had done on the last day of his life, who were his closest friends and associates, and if they knew of any enemies. Natalie let Durwent carry most of it, confining herself to watching this young detective and trying to decide what manner of mind his was. There was keenness here, and quite possibly also ruthlessness: not the sort of man she would want as an antagonist. Yet in a sense that was exactly what he was. Sooner or later he would discover what had been between herself and Will Gregg, and she was not at all sure what his youth would make of a quiet romance between two middle-aged college professors. And slowly her determination grew that no matter what it cost her, Lieutenant Christopher Jensen would not know that she and the dead man had been planning marriage.

"That about does it." Jensen closed his notebook. "You've been helpful. I'm sending out for coffee and doughnuts, unless you'd prefer tea—"

"I'd prefer something stronger than either," Natalie said. "This seems so unreal—"

"It always does."

"I can think of a lot of people," George Durwent said unexpectedly, "whom I'd have thought more likely candidates for murder than Will Gregg—"

Startled, Natalie looked sharply at him. This was not a pronouncement ex cathedra such as the dean was wont to make, and for one moment she almost believed that he had been shaken by Will's death.

"You always can," Jensen agreed, his alert, expressionless eyes flickling quickly from Durwent to Natalie and back. "Even in a world grown used to violence, murder still has the power to shock. Now—would one of you tell me something about Doctor Gregg himself?"

Durwent pulled his glasses from one pocket and a notebook from another. "You understand," he began, "that I haven't the details. That's all in our personnel files at the University."

"At this stage even the sketchiest background will help."

"Ah—well, yes"—the dean studied his notes—"let's see— bachelor of science from Colorado A & M—masters there too, I think—and Ph.D. from Columbia. I believe he still does outside work as a consultant for several firms, one here in town, but the name eludes me."

"Garcia and Sons," Natalie said. "They're contractors."

Durwent scowled at her. "There was a book that has become a standard geology text in high schools. Can you think of anything else, Natalie?"

She shook her head and looked blank, and Jensen suppressed a smile at the dean's visible irritation. "How long was Doctor Gregg on the faculty?" he asked.

"Ah,"—Durwent ruffled the pages of his notebook—"since nineteen-forty-three. Yes. We were lucky to get him during the war."

Jensen looked interested, and the dean grinned nervously. "We weren't contributing to draft evasion, Lieutenant," he said, "Gregg's Four-F status was quite legitimate. I don't know why he had it, he looked perfectly healthy, but it was legal."

18

"Of course you don't know," Natalie snapped, thrusting herself back into what was beginning to seem an unnatural world, "he'd had a touch of TB."

"He never told *me* he was tubercular," Durwent protested.

"He was cured," she answered wearily. "Dr. Raymond Skinner is his physician, Lieutenant, if you want to check."

"I must say, Natalie"—the dean stared balefully at her—"you seem to know a great deal about his private life."

She clenched her fists against the twin-born desire to scream and to strike him. "We've been friends for a long time, George," she managed, "and he'd been a friend of Ben's before our marriage. I don't know what I'd have done without him after Ben was killed. I owe him a great deal," she added simply.

Jensen, watching her, was brushed by a sudden doubt that he could neither recognize nor analyze. Was he fortunate, or the reverse, to have this woman's help? She seemed to feel him watching, and turned to look at him with calm gray-blue eyes.

"You see, Lieutenant," she said, "there may be others more qualified to help, but none who is more obligated."

He nodded silently. "How long had you known Doctor Gregg?"

"Since nineteen-forty-six. Ben—my late husband—had known him since 'thirty-six. Ben was also an archaeologist, and he met Will in New Mexico, where he was helping excavate a pueblo."

"May I know how long your husband's been dead?" Jensen asked, noting that she wore no wedding ring.

"He was killed in World War II, in North Africa. He stepped on a land mine."

Jensen, who had been in Korea, winced.

"Anyhow," she went on, "after I got out of service and finished my doctorate, I started job hunting. Will, whom I knew only by correspondence at that time, recommended me for a job here. I don't know what I'd have done without him. He was the gentlest soul—"

"I'd forgotten you were in service, Natalie," the dean said, "the WAC, wasn't it? Or the Marines?"

"The Air Transport Command. Like lots of qualified women pilots, I ferried airplanes."

Jensen whistled, his admiration for the slender woman suddenly doubling. "Rather dangerous, wasn't it?"

"Not particularly— But aren't we getting off the subject?"

He nodded and consulted his notes. "What about a will? Does either of you know if Doctor Gregg made one, and if so, where it might be?"

"He had one drawn up about a year ago," Natalie told him. "I witnessed it, and he witnessed mine, on the same day. They both favor the scholarship fund, and I think you'll find his in a safe deposit box in the Central Savings Bank."

"Who was the second witness?" Jensen asked.

"Edward Ken, the anthropologist."

"For both wills?"

"Yes."

Jensen finished writing and looked up. "I'm getting the impression that Doctor Gregg often went out of his way to help people."

"He was kind," Natalie agreed, "but not soft. He could be very hard on people whom he thought were using him, or not trying to help themselves. As a matter of fact, he was rather a fanatic on the subject of self-help."

"He certainly was." Durwent re-entered the conversation. "I understand he gave young Archer quite a going over the other day. You know, of course, how *I* feel about Archer. I still say it was a mistake to readmit him."

"I hardly think," Natalie said stiffly, "that this is the time or the place to review our varied philosophies of education."

"Are you suggesting that I'm trying to start an argument?"

"I don't think you ever *try*, George, I think you just manage to start them. Damn it, I don't care how you feel about Peter Archer—all I care about is Will Gregg. He's dead, you know. Someone killed him"—her voice rose suddenly and almost broke—"I don't know how, but someone killed him—"

"I'm sorry." Jensen offered her a cigarette, which she took blindly. "I'd meant to tell you, but—" He looked at the floor between them. "I'm not a doctor, of course, but I'm certain he didn't suffer. He was working at his desk when someone struck him several times at the base of the skull. It was very quick."

Natalie closed her eyes and concentrated on the acrid taste of the smoke in her mouth. Surprisingly, there were no tears to struggle with.

The man who had gone for coffee came back, carrying three paper containers and half a dozen doughnuts wrapped casually in waxed paper. Jensen pulled some pages from his notebook, laid them on Will Gregg's worn but hospitable coffee table, and set the containers on them. Natalie saw and was grateful: his gesture's humanity, its simple considerateness, were at reassuring variance with the brutal presence of murder. Will, to whom courtesy had been instinctive, would have appreciated it.

"Mrs. Keith," Jensen said, unabashedly dunking a doughnut, "you mentioned earlier that Doctor Gregg had had TB. Can you tell me how he contracted it?"

"No. Perhaps Doctor Skinner can."

"When was he last in South America?"

Natalie deliberately finished her coffee and set the empty container on its paper saucer. "I don't know that he ever was."

Jensen looked at her curiously. "Upstairs," he began, "are examples of ancient Indian art and dozens of rock samples labeled as coming from South America. Is it likely that a man would collect such things if he'd never been to the countries involved?"

"I have a splendid Scythian bronze fibula in my collection," she countered, "and I've never seen Lake Aral or the Black Sea."

"Ah, but you're a professional archaeologist."

"And Will was a professional *geo*logist, so your logic comes a cropper, Lieutenant."

"Maybe," he conceded.

A silence rose and held, modified only by the tick of the mantel clock and the passing of an occasional car. Natalie shifted in her chair to ease an aching back and wished she had more coffee.

Why won't they let me see him, she wondered; what are they trying to hide from me? If I could see him—if I could be sure he hadn't suffered— Oh dear God, why? If You exist, how can such things happen?

"Professor Keith," Jensen said suddenly, "you said that Doctor

Gregg met your late husband in the Southwest. If, as you imply, he collected as a hobby, why aren't there any Southwestern Indian relics in his collection? Why, especially if he was friendly with an archaeologist working there, didn't he represent this area?"

"Ben's father," she answered indirectly, "collected stamps, but he hated the British and wouldn't have British stamps in his collection even though they were invented by an Englishman."

"Did Doctor Gregg have an aversion to Southwest Indians?"

His persistence was beginning to annoy her, and she told him so. "I can't see that this is important," she said, "or how it'll help find Will's murderer."

The word was strange on her tongue, and its harsh echo almost drowned Jensen's reply.

"Neither do I at the moment," he agreed placidly, "but it's occurred to me that not even you, Professor, know very much about Wilson Gregg before he joined the faculty of the University."

The dean, long silent, stirred uncomfortably and began to leaf through his notebook. "We have his references on file, Lieutenant, if you want them. All I know is that he lived quietly, did his job well, and was respected in his profession."

"I ask again, Lieutenant," Natalie said impatiently, "is this important now? It's not Will whom you want to arrest—"

"It may be"—Jensen stood up—"and it may not be. What confounds me is that this man, apparently in his late forties, seems not to have existed before the nineteen-forties. And this, after all, is the year of grace, 1960—"

"You know," the dean rumbled on, "it *is* odd. Natalie, you knew him better than I. Didn't he ever tell you about his past?"

She had been braced for the question for some minutes, but now that it had come, she found it difficult to answer. Slowly, with concentration, she chose the words wherewith to explain a man whom she had loved, and who was now dead by violence.

"Will was forty-seven-years old, George," she began. "I'm forty. You, I imagine, are somewhere in between. Can you tell me in perfect honesty that every fact of every year of your adult

22

life is public knowledge? No? Then why be upset about Will? He was a good man."

"He also," Jensen added softly, "has a singularly clever advocate. I'm sorry to keep hounding you good people, but there are still things I've got to do. Now if, as we have reason to believe, the murder was committed during a burglary, recovering the stolen objects can help us find our killer. I'd like you to check upstairs and tell me, if you can, what's missing and if it's potentially salable."

"Will has some valuable pieces," Natalie told him, "but only, I'm afraid, in the artistic and historical sense. There's little of intrinsic worth upstairs."

"Remarkably few art thieves are art experts, Professor," Jensen said. "A lot of 'em just want money for narcotics. I know this won't be pleasant for you, but it has to be done."

He had a way, Natalie reflected as they started upstairs, of phrasing his commands so that obedience seemed to be an act of generosity. It was partly deference, and something else besides: he seemed to know exactly what he was doing and why, and one was drawn to follow him by one's own uncertainty. It was the same quality that, in a Corsican artillery officer and a psychotic Austrian paper hanger, had turned Western civilization upside down and inside out.

CHAPTER II

The long front stairs of Will Gregg's house had a wide mahogany banister so highly polished that Natalie once had jokingly asked him if he slid down it every morning. She remembered this now as she followed the young detective upward. Will had stood, his right hand resting lightly on the head of a Victorian cherub, and had laughed at her. Like many men whose merriment is seldom audible, his laughter had had an exciting, electric quality quite beyond description. Now, without it, the old house seemed alien.

"You may find things out of place in the library," Jensen warned as they approached. "We had to do some moving."

"Was he killed in there?" the dean asked.

"Yes."

The unpremeditated brutality of the question and its casual answer left Natalie nauseated and trembling. She looked down and concentrated on the patterns the toes of her shoes made on the worn maroon rug: right foot, left foot—how had she scuffed the toe of her left shoe?—right foot, left foot—

Will's dead, she told her unbelieving self; Will's been murdered. Oh my God, my God—how can I go on with this?

Jensen nodded to the patrolman at the library door and he opened it. He motioned the dean to go in, but blocked Natalie's way with gentle insistence.

"I think I'd better send you home," he said. "You look rocky."

"It'll be worse if you send me away now," she answered honestly. "Please—just put me to work. I promise not to go hysterical or faint."

He studied her intently, balancing her composure against the gray, haggard look of her face. He had the feeling that she was hurt worse than she wanted anyone—especially him—to know, but she seemed quite in control of herself. Perhaps there had

24

been something between her and Gregg other than friendship. Perhaps there was something about him she didn't want known. Or about herself. He wondered, and the deeper part of his mind reached its intuitive decision and advised him to keep Natalie Keith under observation. He nodded to her.

"He was sitting at his desk," he told her. "Either he didn't hear the murderer come in, or he was expecting someone and ignored him."

"That sounds unlikely, Lieutenant."

"Maybe he was concentrating and just didn't hear."

She nodded and looked beyond him at the deep honey-brown of the oak door. Perhaps the intruder had stood here, in this same place.

"May I see him?" she asked suddenly but with cold calm.

"There's no need," Jensen answered, impersonal but gentle. "We'll ask Doctor Skinner to identify him."

I want to see him, you idiot! she howled silently, I want to see him!

"Yes," she said aloud, "of course. Thank you."

Jensen turned and opened the door. "Like I said," he went on in a conversational tone that jarred Natalie's nerves still more, "we had to do some moving."

She was glad of the warning, though when she stepped into this most personal of Will Gregg's rooms she found that greater violence had been done to its atmosphere than to its appearance. It was a long room, actually two, with the intervening wall knocked out, and overlooked the street. During the day it was light without suffering from glare.

Will's desk, flanked on either side by files, was opposite the door and faced three tall windows. Between these were high, glass-fronted shelves that neatly balanced two similar but larger shelves at the far end of the room. These, and three flat display tables, housed the best of Will Gregg's collection. Across the room, near the door, was the desk used by his secretary, Renata Duval.

In the middle of the room was a long refectory table on which had been spread the clutter of papers and odd specimens usually piled on the desk. A quick appraisal told Natalie that the

25

ancient blotter pad was missing, and she dared not ask why.

"Now what?" George Durwent asked.

"Most of the missing things were in the case nearest the desk," Jensen said. "Take a look and tell me, if you can, what's gone."

"Two Tanagra figurines, a Roman bronze lamp, and the head of an archaic Greek goddess." Natalie spoke without moving. "Also a disputable Etruscan bronze warrior, the neck of a Phoenician amphora, and a small box of Greek and Roman coins."

"How the devil—"

"They, with several of my own pieces," she answered wearily, "are on loan to the Community Art Center."

Jensen's face sagged and took on the aspect of a question mark. "Strange," he muttered, "very strange. Look around—tell me if anything else is missing."

They obeyed, and Natalie, hovering between the desk and the table, caught her breath suddenly and turned to him. "The little gold hammer," she said, "I don't see the little gold hammer."

Jensen scanned his notes. "None was found," he told her. "Can you describe it?"

"Well"—she searched through thickening fatigue for details —"it was a model of a geologist's hammer, about ten inches long, with a gold head about—oh, three or three and a half inches from tip to tip. It was something he won as a student." Her voice caught. "He thought highly of it."

"What kind of head does a geologist's hammer have?" he asked.

Natalie walked to the cases at the far end of the room and knelt to pull out a large drawer. She moved, Jensen noted, with the quick ease of a natural athlete.

"Like this," she said, handing him a full-sized hammer. "One end is a chisel edge, and the other is flat for striking."

"It's square," Jensen mused, hefting the tool and turning it in his hands. For a moment he stood in preoccupied silence, staring at the tool as if it were wholly strange to him.

"This gold model," he asked, "about how large was the square end?"

"Good heavens," Natalie muttered, "the questions! I'd say about half an inch. Why?"

"Because I think it was the murder weapon, that's why."

George Durwent caught his breath. "But it's too small!" he protested, "and too light—"

"It would depend on where the blow landed," Jensen answered. "Thanks for bringing this, Professor. Would you mind putting it back?"

She took it back to its drawer, but remained staring into the display case.

"Something wrong?" Jensen called.

"I don't know," she answered, "but it's certainly odd—"

Jenson came and stood beside her. "What's missing?"

"I'll get the display card," she said, opening the doors. "It seems to have fallen to the next shelf. What's gone is a small, late dynastic Egyptian bronze of a falcon, the totem bird of the god Horus. I found it years ago, in Nubia. Will always admired it, so I gave it to him last Christmas."

"Have you any idea how long it's been missing?"

"It was here this noon. As I told you earlier, I had lunch with Will, and I remember looking at Horus and thinking that he was getting what's known as 'bronze disease' and needed some work done."

"Maybe Will sent it to the museum lab," Durwent suggested.

She shook her head. "I didn't mention it."

"Knowing women," Durwent said sourly, "you probably did."

"Tell me," Jensen interrupted, "was this bird solid, or hollow?"

"Hollow," Natalie answered, "but I assure you the ancient Egyptians didn't hide gems or narcotics in their religious hardware."

"No, but there are plenty of moderns who might."

Stunned, Natalie swung around and faced him. "Are you insinuating—" she began.

"No," he answered gently, "I don't think Doctor Gregg was a fence or a pusher. But whoever killed him may be." He reached out and took the display card from her. "By the way, what do the letters 'N.L.K.' mean?"

27

"My initials," she answered. "My maiden name was Lethbridge."

"Did Doctor Gregg always put the finder's initials on his specimens?"

There was a peculiar guilelessness in his voice that Natalie was beginning to mistrust as a harbinger of loaded questions. "Well," she hedged, "I couldn't say. He did sometimes, but why, I couldn't guess—"

"Something's missing here!" Durwent called from across the room. "The card says 'Cylinder Seal, L.M.II or III'—whatever *that* means!—'from Hagia Triada.'"

"Oh dear," Natalie gasped, *"mea culpa, Legate, mea culpa!* I borrowed it for a lecture last spring and never returned it."

"And what," Jensen asked politely, "does L.M.II or III mean?"

"Late Minoan era, second or third phase," she answered. "It's a well-preserved piece, though the workmanship's nothing to rave about."

Jensen stood digesting this and other facts. "Funny," he said finally, "I'd been thinking of this as an Indian collection."

"Indian work does dominate," Natalie agreed, "it's bold and it's colorful."

"And entirely misleading to the laity." He smiled. "Take that old textile. Can you tell me anything about it? I have a good friend who weaves."

"Well," she said, "it's Peruvian, from the Nazca culture, which is pre-Inca. More than that I can't say, except that it should be under glass. There's too much sulfur in the air here."

"Your field's the Middle East, isn't it?" he asked. "I seem to recall a book—"

Natalie smiled, and realized that the fine muscles of her face had been set tautly. "I started in Egyptology, with Ben, but I've dug in what's now Israel, nosed around Mycenae, and made a dreadful nuisance of myself on Crete."

"Have you ever worked in this country?"

"Oh yes. We take students into the field almost every summer. A couple of years ago we got as far away as Alaska."

"Hadn't we better get back to the inventory?" the dean suggested.

"It might be a good idea," Jensen agreed. "Let's see—the things from the case are on loan"—he frowned at his notebook—"which means that the only thing honestly missing is the bronze bird."

"Hawk," Natalie corrected automatically. "That does awful things to your robbery motive, doesn't it?"

"It doesn't help," Jensen admitted, "unless there was something in the desk. Mrs. Keith, are you *sure* Doctor Gregg wasn't involved in anything secret?"

"Spies and intrigues?" the dean asked, startled.

"In a way," he answered. "Businesses have been known to maintain intelligence systems much like governments."

"Espionage," Natalie said, "but not murder."

The door to the library opened abruptly, and all three turned in surprise as a tall, heavy-set man thrust himself into the room. "Ooops, sorry, Chris! I thought you were alone."

"It's all right, Turk," he said, "come in. Have you finished with Gregg's secretary?"

The man called Turk came and sat heavily on the edge of the long table. "Either that," he said, "or she's finished with me. Why didn't you tell me she was a nut?"

"Is she?"

"Probably not certifiable, but pretty far out. You know—horoscopes, little friends in the 'great beyond'—that sort of jazz. She just doesn't seem the type to work for a college professor."

"Ah, the Duval charm!" Natalie said, "it never fails. She comes from New Orleans, Lieutenant, and claims to have Indian blood that gives her assorted occult powers. Edward Ken—he's an anthropologist—finds her fascinating."

"Professor Keith"—Jensen bowed slightly—"meet Detective Sergeant Cyrus Harrison, better known as Turk."

The sergeant smiled amiably and got to his feet. Dean Durwent sneezed, was hastily remembered, and also introduced.

"Where's the Duval woman now?" Jensen asked. "Did you send her home?"

"Nope." Harrison shook his head. "She wants to see you."

"Me?"

"You're the 'man in charge,'" Harrison said. "Serves you right, I guess. Shall I get her?"

Jensen nodded and watched silently as his partner went to the door, opened it, and nodded to the woman who waited outside.

"The lieutenant'll see you now, Miss Duval," he said. "Come in."

She came to the threshold and stopped. Watching, Natalie was struck for the first time by her height.

There's something of the Valkyrie in her, she thought; Creole-Indian blood or not. I wish she wasn't wearing red—it seems so out of place.

"Come in, Miss Duval," Jensen said. "I think you know the Professor and Dean Durwent—"

"I know them," Renata Duval answered.

"Then come in and tell me what's troubling you."

"I can't. A man has died in this room."

Jensen looked quickly at Natalie, and then away again. "He's not here now, Miss Duval. Come in—"

"You don't understand, Officer. I am a sensitive, and if there is a restless spirit present—"

"You mean you're a medium?"

"If you prefer that term, yes. I shall speak to you from here."

Jensen nodded. "If you wish," he said.

Renata Duval inclined her head in acknowledgment. "I have had a telegram from my brother-in-law in New Orleans," she said. "My sister is ill, and he wants me to come. There is a young child. This other officer has said I must stay here, but I have told him everything I know."

Jensen turned to Harrison. "Sergeant?" he asked.

"Yes, sir," Harrison answered, "Miss Duval has been very co-operative. I was thinking of the future—you know, the things that crop up to surprise you. As Doctor Gregg's secretary, Miss Duval probably knows more about him and his affairs than anyone else."

30

"But I *have* to go!" Renata Duval interrupted. "My sister is to be operated on, on Saturday. She has cancer—"

"I'm not inhuman, Miss Duval," Jensen said, "but I am a police officer investigating a homicide."

"I'm not stupid," Renata Duval snapped, "I know what you're doing. But my sister has a young child, and her husband works all day. Must the living suffer for the dead?"

Natalie gasped, and Jensen unconsciously reached toward her. "Some of the living always do, Miss Duval; but I understand how you feel. How long would you be in New Orleans?"

"The operation is Saturday," she said. "We should know one way or the other within a week."

"It's irregular"—Jensen scrawled a note to remind himself to check the address—"and I'll have the devil's own time justifying it, but I'll let you go. Give the information to Sergeant Harrison, so we can reach you. I hope," he added grimly, "you won't make it necessary for the New Orleans police to send you back if I need you."

Renata Duval nodded again. "You have my word."

"When do you plan to leave?"

"Tonight. I have a reservation on the two-thirty plane."

"You haven't much time." Jensen checked his watch. "Sergeant, get the information and then have Cohen drive Miss Duval to the airport."

She made her half bow for the last time, nodded to Natalie and the dean, and left. Harrison went with her, and returned a few minutes later.

"All clear, Turk?" Jensen asked.

"I hope so. Want a rundown?"

"It would be helpful."

Harrison grinned and fumbled in his pocket for his notebook. "Deceased had no classes yesterday," he read, "worked here with Duval until eleven forty-five. Had luncheon guest whom Duval 'declined' to identify, though I'm sure she knows who it was."

"So do I." Jensen smiled. "It was Mrs. Keith."

Harrison lifted an eyebrow and went on. "Deceased had an appointment downtown at four with Garcia and Sons, which he kept. Another appointment at eight-thirty with someone named Archer."

Natalie and the dean turned simultaneously to stare at him.

"Did you say Archer?" Durwent demanded.

"Steady on, George," Natalie advised, "there must be fifty Archers in the phone book. There are four among the student body."

"That's interesting," Jensen said. "With which of them did Doctor Gregg have an argument the other day?"

"Peter Archer," Durwent answered, crossing the room and standing close to him, "a sophomore who was readmitted against my advice after a year's absence. Everyone was against him but Natalie, Will Gregg, and Edward Ken."

"But," Jensen said, flipping pages in his notebook, "a while ago you said that Doctor Gregg had 'given him quite a going over.' Why?"

"For failing two mid-semester examinations," Durwent snapped. "I told them the boy was no good, but no—they had to give him another chance! He just isn't college material."

"That's a pretty sweeping statement," Jensen said quietly. "How do you mean it?"

"The usual." Durwent shrugged. "Poor family background, public-school education of no great quality, and no life goal at all. I feel that the University has an obligation to the individual, Lieutenant, but I also think the group is more important. After all, man *is* a social being. Archer is a loner—"

"Yes," Natalie said with a coldness that raised the hair on the back of Jensen's neck, "he brings us nothing but the curiosity of a young puppy and an I.Q. of a hundred and forty-five. He's got a tough, original mind, and he was willing to give his right arm for an education."

For the first time Jensen realized that Natalie Keith's subtle —and unsubtle—thrusts at the dean were neither intended in humor nor were the by-products of jangled nerves. The difference between these two was almost as deep as it was wide, and the shadow of Peter Archer seemed to be the measure of it. With sinking spirit Jensen realized that he might have to accept

32

the dean's psychological geometry and his statement that Archer was "no good."

"What's Archer's major?" Harrison asked.

"Mr. Archer"—the dean snorted—"hasn't seen fit to confine himself to an organized discipline."

"Professor?"

When she answered, it was with hesitation. "There are a dozen ways to describe Peter, and every one's a cliché. He's a new canvas, an unexposed film, a new day—in short, Sergeant, a throwback to the Renaissance—a man who aspires to know everything, and has yet to learn that he never will."

"A moment ago," Harrison probed "you said he was 'willing to give his right arm for an education.' Exactly what did you mean?"

"Just what I said," Natalie answered. "Peter worked in a factory for two years before matriculating, and he went back the summer after his freshman year. An hydraulic press backfired or something, and took his right arm off almost to the elbow."

"Well," Harrison sighed, "that shoots *that* idea. Now what, Chris?"

"Who knows?" Jensen muttered, taking a sheaf of pages from his notebook. "Leave these at the office, will you? and have 'em typed. Is there a stapler anywhere, Mrs. Keith?"

"There's a large praying mantis on the filing cabinet. Staplers," she added in hasty explanation, "always remind me of praying mantises."

Harrison rubbed his chin. "There is a resemblance."

Jensen, scowling in annoyance, turned the stapler upside down and peered at the barrel. "I don't care if it looks like a purple kangaroo," he growled, "it's jammed."

"That's odd, it's always worked before. Give it to me; maybe I can fix it. There's a trick someone showed me—"

"Never mind, professor," Jensen said, setting the stapler down with the rest of the things from Will Gregg's desk. "I'll make do with a clip. If you see the inspector, Turk, tell him this one isn't as simple as it looked."

Harrison left, and it occurred to Natalie that he walked

lightly for so bulky a man. She found it intriguing that two such physically opposite types should be teamed together. Harrison was dark and craggy, and Jensen viking fair and lithe: a football lineman and a sprinter.

"Well," Jensen sighed, "have you two found anything else missing?"

"No," the dean answered, "but my acquaintance with Doctor Gregg was entirely professional."

"Well," Natalie shot back, "I should hope so!"

Attack and riposte, Jensen thought; very neat.

"Mrs. Keith?"

"Nothing," she said, "and that seems odd. There's a rough diamond here the size of a marble, plainly labeled, and even if it's not a gem stone, it would bring a good price in industry."

"Anything else?"

Her expression didn't change, nor did she move, but her eyes flashed up to meet the detective's and hold them. She knew then that he was testing her for some reason of his own, and that she had moved too deeply into the search for Will Gregg's killer ever to be free until it was ended.

"As a matter of fact," she heard herself say, "there's one strange thing. Most of the South American specimens have Will's initials on them."

"'W.A.G.,'" Jensen read, leaning over the display table. "I was wondering about that. What's the A for?"

"He never used his middle name," Natalie explained, "which isn't surprising, since it was Athelstan."

"A lot of men," Jensen said with hurt dignity, "are named for their grandfathers."

She blinked. "How did you know?"

"*I* got stuck with Oscar."

"Good God!"

"Well"—Jensen smiled, grateful for the distraction—"that seems to be all we can do tonight. I'll be in touch with you both later about formal statements. May I drive you home, Mrs. Keith?"

Natalie looked at her watch and shook her head. "Thanks, but it's so late now that if I go home, I'll never make it to

34

my first class. I'll wander over to my office and read or check papers until the cafeteria opens."

Jensen nodded. "I'll send a man with you. How about you, Dean Durwent? May I drop you somewhere?"

"Why yes," he answered, "thank you. I have a theory I'd like to discuss with you—in private."

"That'll be fine, sir." Jensen nodded absently. "Are you sure you'll be all right, Mrs. Keith?"

"It's kind of you to be concerned, Lieutenant," she said, "but there's no cause. I'll be better off at the office, working, than home, thinking."

He nodded. "You may be right. I'll call you sometime tomorrow, if it's all right, and thanks for your help tonight."

CHAPTER III

Inevitable, Natalie Keith thought as she sat in the silence of her office; inevitable, inexorable, omnipresent. The history of the human race in one four-letter word—pain. We learn it as children, live with it as adults, and bow down to it in our age. Oh God, why do I go on? I've already outlived everyone I ever loved.

In that other time, when Ben Keith had fallen to the impersonal but intimate violence of war, she had sought escape and had found it in her work. Not consciously at first, but later with increasing deliberateness, she had marshaled the powers of her mind and bade them labor: to arrange, to analyze, to synthesize, to criticize—in short, to erect a tight realm of scholarship wherein there was no chance for those whom she cared for to be hurt or broken; to play at being a god of the Olympian sort who will have his way or hurl a peevish bolt.

Those who had guided her to her doctorate had agreed that she was gifted, but suspected that she might also be ruthless. Those whom she had taught in her early years had concluded that she was ruthless and suspected that she was brilliant. Only one man had bothered to seek out the lonely thing behind the barricade of facts and artifacts: only Will Gregg had cared to know Natalie Keith. But for him, the defense might in time have become impregnable.

He had neither wanted nor willed a change in her, but he had wrought it. He had borne her remoteness, her self-centeredness, her outright ill temper, until with time she had come to trust him. Why or how, she had never understood, except that he lived unashamedly by the Christian faith she had long since discarded as untenable. And now Will Gregg was dead, uselessly and needlessly, by the hand of a fellow human being.

36

And his god let it happen, she thought; this god whom he said was love allowed him to be killed. But Will was no fool —no, if there's meaning to life—and death—you won't find it in that direction. You won't find it in the past or in the future, either. You'll find it right here and now.

In the last of the foredawn moments she recognized the war within herself. The old instinct to retreat was strong, and the new one, the bewildering sense that to do so was both wrong and disloyal, left her too confused to think. She could, of course, still retire to the old pattern, or she could accept the circumstance that had caught her up in the search for Will's murderer and become more and more deeply involved with human tragedy and failing. The choice lay before her as clear-cut as the ink spots on her desk blotter, and she knew that such an involvement, once accepted, would not end when a jury was dismissed or a judge passed sentence. On the one hand was relief of pain and a long, ever-deepening anesthesia that would end only with her own death; on the other, more hurt, more disappointment, more sorrow and what Will had called "the fugitive thing named peace."

No, she thought, not now. I must work, I must have something to cling to until I can think again. At least history is beyond the reach of change. At least the past is stable.

With ninety per cent of her consciousness, Natalie applied herself to the folder of term papers that had brooded for days in the middle of her desk. "Indications of Foreign Influence in the Neolithic Pottery of Lower Egypt"—"The Importance of the Minoan and Mycenaean Empires in the Formation of European Civilization"—"Current Views on the Location of King Nestor's Palace at Pylos"—where, she wondered, despairing, was the dividing line between scholarship and pedantry, between originality and imitation? How could minds theoretically equal and at the same stage of development produce work so appallingly dissimilar? What was it in the human spirit that made one mind content to assemble and quote while another, no better equipped, dared grab beyond its reach for ideas that glittered in the light of speculation? Did contentment preclude courage, or was it the other way around?

No, she thought, shoving the papers aside; I can't cope with this now. If I try I'll go mad—unless I am already. Oh God, which is the real world? What do I care what these children think about Badarian pots or the Minoan empire? I've lost Will . . .

She had met Ben Keith when her father decided to celebrate her winning a college scholarship by taking his whole family on a Mediterranean cruise. She had already announced her intention to study archaeology, and he had arranged a visit to a dig in Egypt, hoping perhaps that the heat, the hard work and primitive living conditions would change her mind. But he had been mistaken in this, just as he was when he concluded that one flying lesson would be enough. She had stayed in Egypt while the rest of her family "did" Palestine and the Greek islands. The dig director, Hugh Laurence—now the redoubtable Sir Hugh who terrorized Oxford undergraduates—finally had sent her to rejoin her kin with his grudging but sincere approval. Two years later, after a year at Oxford, she and Ben Keith had been married in Athens. She had been nineteen and he twenty-two, and the year had been nineteen-thirty-nine.

In their wonder at each other, they had refused to admit the chaos that grew about them. Even after it had begun, wedge-like, to drive them apart, somehow they had maintained their oneness. Then Ben was killed, and she, still young enough to hope in the future, had steadied herself by finishing the book he had begun.

But she was no longer young, and she knew that the remainder of her life would be much as the past had been: a succession of minor triumphs and minor failures, a rolling plane unrelieved by either mountains or valleys. Work had become a burden that flayed old scars, and gradually, in the silent and empty office, the scholar and teacher yielded to the woman who could only suffer. She turned off her lamp and sat in darkness, struggling against the unbelievable truth that was too obvious to deny: Will Gregg was dead, and there would not again be the sound of his voice or the deep, pervading joy of his nearness.

Outside it was just coming dawn, and the campus lay in the

38

stillness peculiar to the hour. The grass, let go shaggy with the end of September, showed pearl-gray with hoarfrost. It too had died, and ahead lay only the long sterility of winter. The leaves of the dogwood that she and Will had watched blossom, leaf out, and finally turn an antique red, had fallen and lay scattered, their borrowed elements already returning to the earth that had nurtured them. When spring came, if spring came, there would be new leaves dressing a world that would be, for her, also new and strange.

If I could weep, she thought, then perhaps I could sleep. I'm so tired—so terribly tired.

Absently, as if her hands possessed volition of their own, she opened her desk drawer, took out a small object, and began to roll it compulsively between her fingers. She ought, she decided, to try once more with the term papers.

With sudden resolution she snapped on her light, pulled the folder back to her, and opened it. She looked down, expecting to see the stub of a pencil in her fingers, and saw instead a cylinder of gray-green stone—the Minoan seal that was missing from Will Gregg's collection. She stared at it, and the long-desired tears began to flow. Silently, without violence or passion, she wept for her dead. As the first of the day's electrum sunlight touched the ground outside, she cradled her head in her arm and slept.

It was a small, familiar sound that roused her, the sound of a key in a lock. Natalie sat up, her back aching and her shoulders stiff, and tried to remember where she was. She looked around just in time to see the outer door of the office swing slowly open as the department secretary, deep in conversation with an unseen friend, arrived reluctantly at work. Mercifully, she paused long enough to give Natalie time to order her thoughts and get up from her desk.

"Good morning, Jeanne," she said.

The girl started sharply and looked around, her face blank with surprise. "Professor Keith! Oh dear—"

Natalie smiled, put the cylinder seal gently back in the

drawer, and pushed it closed. "Is the cafeteria open? I'm terribly hungry."

"Well, yes," Jeanne stammered, "that is—I guess it is. When did you—I mean, how long have you been here?"

Natalie shrugged. "Since about five. I started to grade papers and fell asleep."

Surprise gave way to worry and finally to an expression of acute uneasiness, and Jeanne stood uncertainly between the office door and her own desk. "I don't suppose," she began tentatively, "that you've seen the papers or heard the radio—"

"It's all right, child," Natalie said gently, "I know about Doctor Gregg. The dean and I spent most of the night with the police."

"Oh." Jeanne's relief, compassion, and curiosity were oddly mixed in her expression. "Is it true what the papers said? Was he murdered?"

Natalie, finding to her dismay that she could not speak, nodded curtly and started toward the door. "If Professor Goldman comes while I'm in the cafeteria, tell him I'm here, and under no circumstances is he to cancel my lectures. By the way, do you have that book list ready?"

"Yes, ma'am."

"Thank you." Natalie tried hard to smile. "And another thing —I'm not available to anyone except the police and people I already have appointments with. This thing could get out of hand—"

"Yes, ma'am," Jeanne said again.

It was an absurd line to exit on, Natalie knew, but she did nothing to change it. Jeanne would think her singularly hard and without feeling, but it might be better so. The old ways could still provide some shelter.

From the moment she left the office she became aware of a curious tension in the atmosphere of the University. By the time she got downstairs and saw the swarm of faculty and students in the hall by the cafeteria, she was oppressed by it. She was moved to change her mind, cancel her classes and go home, but decided she could not. She had already passed

40

the point of no return, she thought, and then wondered why her mind was suddenly snapping at clichés.

As she started toward the place where the line was organizing she had a vague impression of being preceded by a wave of silence. The crowd seemed somehow to draw back from her, though she saw no overt motion. Perhaps it was only her own sense of loss, of isolation, which made it seem so, and she told herself that she could prove it by walking up to the nearest cluster of people and joining their conversation. Unfortunately, the nearest to hand was comprised of an assistant professor of English whom she disliked, and a graduate student whom she didn't know.

". . . I wonder how Natalie Keith is taking it," the assistant professor was saying, "she's a tough old bird, but still—"

The graduate student looked up with an expression somewhere between a smirk and a leer, and then went rigid.

The assistant professor turned. "My dear Natalie," he said, rallying quickly, "I'm so sorry—such a *terrible* loss for you—"

"Do you regret the loss, Doctor Tasman," she asked stiffly, "or my intrusion on your little tête-a-tête?"

"I—eh—" Tasman looked desperately to the graduate student, who ignored him. "Oh, what the hell, Natalie."

"Your manners are atrocious," she said bitterly, "but your sense of direction is excellent. Were you planning a trip?"

"Now look here," he flashed, "you'll have to admit that you and Gregg—"

" 'Admit?' " she demanded. " 'Admit' what? Make an accusation for once, Doctor Tasman, and see if I admit anything."

He hesitated, then pounced on a single phrase. "Just what are you implying by that 'for once' remark, Professor? Are you trying to suggest—"

"I'm not *trying*." Her anger was immediate and alive. "I haven't lived with campus gossip for all these years without figuring out where it starts. You obviously enjoy spreading vicious and cruel stories, Doctor, but have you any friends left? Or do you fancy yourself another Alexander Pope? You're not, you know. You're a second-rate scholar with a gutter mind and a tongue that should be boiled."

She was hot and shivering at the same moment, wanting to lash out at him physically as well as verbally, but unable to do so. She, who had never consciously hated, realized with sudden clarity that the emotion, far from being new, was actually only the logical culmination of the many resentments she had harbored through the years.

Tasman, shocked and confused, hesitated before reacting. It was not that she was never angry—she was, with fair frequency—but he had never seen her in the sort of rage that struck without direction. Witless aggression was as alien to Natalie Keith as feathers to a fish.

"Now look," he began, unconsciously retreating before her, "you'd better have proof before you say things like that before witnesses."

"Why don't you sue me for libel?" she suggested coldly, "if you dare—"

"You're out of your mind!"

"I'd enjoy it," she went on, ignoring him, "but I don't think you would. In fact, it might be the end of you."

"What about yourself?" Tasman challenged, seizing the chance to put her on the defensive, "it'd finish you too."

"I've nothing to hide," she said, her anger solidifying to cold, hard fury, "nor have I ambition to feed. I can afford to take chances."

A firm hand on her elbow drew her away from her antagonist before either of them could speak again. When she finally looked up, it was to see the irregular, bearded face of Edward Ken, the anthropologist, beside her. The faculty's "odd man out" had come to her rescue.

"Wow!" the graduate student gasped.

"My boy," Tasman said triumphantly, just loudly enough for Natalie to hear, "you have just witnessed what could be a classic interpretation of Medea—"

"Not all barbarians," Edward Ken observed judiciously, watching Natalie's struggle not to respond, "wear bones in their noses. Lester Tasman is a little cannibal, and everyone knows it. Shall I see you through the food line, my dear, or vanish?"

"I'm not hungry. In fact, I feel sick."

"I know," Ken answered, "but one has an obligation to the body. Believe me, Natalie, food now will make the rest of the day more bearable."

"Simple, sensible, and to the point." She half smiled. "Thank you, Edward."

He shook his head and smiled ruefully. "There's an old Latin motto you should know—*Illegitami non Carborundum*. Don't let the bastards grind you down, Nat."

"I won't," she promised, her voice catching, "but I'm glad I have the afternoon off."

He reached out, took a tray from the stack, and handed it to her. "Eat sensibly, if not with gusto," he advised kindly. "Call us tonight, old girl—"

He left, and she ate hurriedly and alone, realizing for the first time in her life how it felt to have people deliberately avoid her eyes or evade her company. By the time she got back to her desk she had conceived a burgeoning contempt for everything and everyone connected with the University. It was to be expected that the young should regard Will's death as exciting and herself as a woman of mystery, but that her colleagues—

By an act of will she quashed her resurgent anger at Lester Tasman and remembered Edward Ken and his kindness. It was true that not all barbarians wore bones in their noses: neither, she reminded herself, were all scholars civilized.

At nine o'clock, in a mood of peculiar bitterness, she went to lecture on the life and times of Socrates.

CHAPTER IV

Detective Lieutenant Christopher Oscar Jensen got four hours' sleep on a cot at police headquarters, shaved with a borrowed razor, and had the odd privilege of overhearing two veteran detectives wondering out loud how "the boy wonder" would do on his first homicide case. And because he was not at all sure how, or even what, he would do, he sat for a time in his office and stared at his neatly typed notes from the night before.

Obviously he could rule out an art thief as the murderer. A call to the Community Art Center had established that Doctor Gregg's missing pieces were indeed on loan there, together with several belonging to Doctor Natalie Keith. The small amount of cash in the house—not more than fifty dollars, judging by the state of his bank account—on the face of it made robbery an unlikely motive.

Yet the house had been entered and Gregg murdered. Jensen chewed on a pencil and then began to write. The possibilities as he saw them were four: an itinerant homicidal maniac; an ordinary burglar who killed in fear or frustration or both; industrial espionage; and, finally, personal grudge. Of these, number one was manifestly improbable, and number two unlikely since Gregg had been sitting at his own desk when he was killed. That left numbers three and four, and of these, spying seemed the more likely. Illogical, perhaps, but possible. After all, the man was a geologist, and it was known that he had worked as a consultant for a number of oil and mining companies.

As for the fourth possibility, Jensen considered it briefly and withheld judgment; hatred, like greed and fear, was in some degree a motive in every act of violence. It would be interesting to know how Professor Keith, as an historian, felt about it.

At eleven-twenty Turk Harrison appeared with a detailed list

44

of the effects and possessions of the deceased, and with a sheaf of facts and opinions gleaned from his colleagues and employers. He also brought coffee, which was the most appreciated of all.

Wilson Athelstan Gregg had not been a genius, but beneath an impressive structure of knowledge there had been a capacity for imaginative and flexible thought that had nurtured in many the suspicion that he was awesomely close to it. A field engineer employed by Garcia and Sons stated that Gregg's advice on subsurface rock structure was usually uncannily accurate. An oil-company executive (called, at city expense, by long distance) testified to his shrewd interpretation of seismographic explorations, while from a New York publisher, who gave the impression of being on the verge of shock, the placid Harrison had received an emotional report of Gregg's gifts as a teacher, editor, and writer.

"He must have been quite a guy," Harrison concluded.

"Oh? Whatever gave you that idea?"

Harrison fanned his notes like a bridge hand. "Look at these. You know those egghead types as well as I do, Chris. They're articulate—downright glib, sometimes—and jealous as all hell of anyone on their own level. But there's none of that with Gregg. They liked him. They honestly liked him."

"With two exceptions, you're right," Jensen said.

Harrison studied him for a moment. "Exception number one being the murderer, but who's number two?"

"George Durwent, doctor of education," Jensen answered, "and he doesn't like Professor Keith, either. He even advised me to have her investigated."

"Maybe he doesn't like himself," Harrison suggested.

"Maybe not. This whole thing is a pretty convincing picture, Turk, but part of it is a forgery."

"So what're we going to do about it?"

The question was relentlessly practical, and Jensen shrugged and tossed his empty coffee container neatly into the wastepaper basket. "I don't know. Maybe get my head examined. I'm becoming a terribly suspicious character."

"I know the feeling." Harrison grinned and handed him a

book of matches to light his cigarette. "You keep wondering what the hell you've overlooked."

Jensen grunted and blew out a cloud of smoke, almost reaching the point of admitting to himself that he had been happier in the Twelfth Precinct than he was in Central Homicide. "I don't suppose," he asked tentatively, "that there's any indication of Gregg's being involved in anything secret for any business firm or—Heaven forbid!—the government?"

"I've got men checking it out now, Chris."

Jensen stared at the burning end of the cigarette. "I hope that's the answer. It'd be nice, for once, to have a storybook ending."

The sergeant, his senior in service if not in years, gave him a searching look and was silent for a time. "You're a funny kind of cop, Chris," he said eventually.

"Yeah, aren't I?"

"You're thinking about Professor Keith, aren't you?"

"As the dean pointed out in detail and with relish, she knows more than she's telling."

Harrison grunted and tugged at his ear. "Gregg had an appointment with Garcia at four o'clock and kept it. He also had one with Peter Archer at eight-thirty. So the question is, where was the lady professor at nine?"

Jensen shot him an intense, almost resentful look. "About the Archer kid—have you checked him out yet?"

"I was hoping you'd ask that," Harrison said, "I talked with his roommate at South Hall, and came up with the following. One—Archer flunked two exams last week. Two—this annoyed Gregg, who'd taken an interest in the boy. Three—Archer's roommate was out when Archer got home last night, and when he got in about ten forty-five, he found Archer working on his second beer and in a lousy mood, contemplating his artifical arm, which was broken. Archer'd been drinking that afternoon too."

"What about the arm?"

"I brought it along." Harrison produced a bundle wrapped in newspaper and handed it to Jensen.

Jensen tried hard to swallow his excitement, opened the bundle and spread a complex of metal, plastic, and white nylon webbing on his desk. It was indeed quite thoroughly out of commission.

"How's he supposed to have done this, Turk?"

"Changing a flat tire."

"Which means heavy work with tools." Jensen squinted at a dark smudge on plastic socket. "Where's Archer now?"

"Home for the weekend."

"He likes 'em long. It's only Thursday."

"I see I have made my point."

Jensen picked up the artificial arm and studied it. The dark stains could be, probably were, grease. But to break a metal hook as this one was broken, to shear it off clean, would require considerable force—more than enough force to hammer in the back of a man's head.

He hefted the prosthesis and pondered it silently. "Listen to me," he said finally, "and answer me not until I have emptied my thoughts."

Harrison gave him a strange look. "I think those Ph.D.s are affecting you, Chris."

"Be still, knave! Allow me my whimsy—"

"Be my guest!"

Jensen ignored him, and reviewed his four theories of the motive for the murder. "I'd say it was a tossup between industrial spying gone wrong, and revenge, with perhaps some inclination toward revenge at this stage. As Dorothy Sayers put it in some book or other, opportunity can be more important than motive in finding a murderer, and from where I sit Peter Archer has both."

"But the boy's an amputee—"

"Awkward, I'll admit," Jensen said, "but I don't think it eliminates him."

"I don't follow you, Chris."

"I'm not sure I follow me, either," Jensen said with a sigh, "but I think we've got to start with the best suspect we have, and that's Archer."

"What about Professor Keith?"

"Put someone on it. But I'd say Archer's the best bet."

"If we can find him."

"We'll find him."

"He's had hours of clean time," Harrison pointed out.

"And he gets more the longer we stand here arguing. Get someone on it, Turk, and then check to see if anything's come in on that missing gold hammer."

Harrison nodded and turned to leave, almost knocking down another detective who commented bitterly on overweight policemen and handed Jensen a large Manila envelope. Jensen, his mind still centered on the broken machine on his desk, took the document casually and found inside a covering memorandum addressed to himself.

To: Det. Lt. C. O. Jensen, Homicide

From: Oliver Harrup, M.D., Office of the County Medical Examiner

Re: POST MORTEM ON W. A. GREGG

Death was cause by massive intercranial hemorrhage involving the cerebellum and respiratory center. A simple skull fracture was noted in conjunction with extensive surface contusions and bruising from repeated blows by an instrument, about one-half inch square and with sharp edges. There was considerable external bleeding, but this was not, in our opinion, a contributing factor in death.

Time of death is estimated as between 9:30 and 10:00 P.M. The injuries noted above could have been inflicted by a right-handed person standing behind and slightly to the left of the deceased.

Jensen breathed deeply, blessing Doctor Harrup as he did, and exhaled slowly. He dropped the report on his desk, picked up the telephone, and dialed Urban Hospital.

"Extension two-five-seven, please," he said.

The phone rang several times, and then, against a background of miscellaneous noise, a woman's voice announced, "Occupational Therapy, Miss Patton speaking—"

"Lieutenant Jensen, Police Department. Is Miss Andrews there, please?"

"Oh gosh," the voice said, "what's she done? Hang on a minute, I'll get her."

The ill-assorted racket came to an abrupt halt, and he could hear voices dimly in the sudden still. "Chris," another woman asked, "what're you trying to do, anyhow? You've just scared our student out of ten years' growth."

"Tell her I'm from Homicide and scare her out of twenty," he suggested lightly. "I need your help, Laura. If I come over, can you get free in, say—half an hour?"

"Only for something dreadfully official."

"It's the Gregg case. You heard it on the news, probably."

Laura caught her breath audibly. "Is that one yours? When you get here, page me and I'll meet you in the office."

"Okay." he smiled. "This'll be the first time I've seen you at work—"

"Down, boy," she advised, and hung up.

He grinned at the dead phone, and then looked up to see Turk Harrison standing in the doorway.

"What's that all about?" he asked.

"Expert witness," Jensen answered gruffly. "Anything on the hammer?"

"Nope."

"Damn! Look, Turk—I want every inch of Gregg's house gone over again. Including the grounds. Then I want every possible route to South Hall covered and searched—trash cans, sewers, mail boxes, the works."

"What about South Hall itself?"

"It goes without saying."

Harrison grinned with pure malice. "Looks like a busy day for the uniformed boys."

"Doesn't it just?" Jensen agreed. "I'm going over to Urban Hospital to talk to my witness, and then, so help me! I'm going home and get some sleep. I suggest you do the same."

"I'm planning to," Harrison answered. "See you tomorrow."

Natalie Lethbridge Keith, archaeologist, teacher, and pilot, finished her day's lectures and left the University. But she did not go home. Instead she took a bus northward through city and suburb to the municipal airport. There, in a borrowed airplane, she sought consolation in a Lowery sky that forewarned of snow and turbulence to come. For two hours she occupied the same few miles of air, putting the plane through precise and complex maneuvers until her mind, nerves, and muscles seemed fused with the controls. In the gray world of air there were only herself and the steady, reassuring throb of the engine, and she stayed until, her fuel exhausted, the pull of earth obliged her to return and land.

Her telephone was ringing as she opened her apartment door, and she wondered if she would ever hear the sound again without a prick of fear. After a moment of debating whether or not to answer, she did.

"Yes?" she asked, hoping vaguely that it was a wrong number.

"Professor Keith?"

"Yes. Who is this?"

"Chris Jensen. I've been trying to get you for hours. Where've you been, anyhow?"

"Oh," she temporized, "up in the air. Is something wrong?"

"I don't think so, but I'd like to talk to you. Have you had supper?"

"Supper?" she repeated as if the idea were new. "Good Lord, I haven't even had lunch!"

"Well then, I'll be by in half an hour and we'll split the difference. I really do want to talk to you."

She gave up protesting before she even tried. "You don't give a person much choice, do you, Lieutenant?"

"Why, Professor," he answered, "ours is a very democratic police force! See you in half an hour."

Natalie, who had wanted only a hot bath and some sleep, compromised on a hot bath and a change of clothes and went down to meet Jensen. She did not want to go out to eat: she had done everything she could think of to wear herself out so that she could sleep, and now she must find the energy to be reasonably polite and intelligent to a detective. She watched Jensen pull up in front of her building and resented him with a vehemence that startled her.

"Am I late?" he asked, getting out to meet her.

"As a matter of fact," she answered stiffly, "yes."

He opened the door for her, then came back and slid behind the wheel. "Dean Durwent is conveniently sick, so I have a good excuse to talk to you instead. He's—ah—rather overwhelming, isn't he?"

His tone amused her, and thereby increased her annoyance. "I remember the first time I saw him," she recalled, "he was coming across campus in full academic robes. There was a wind blowing, and he looked like a square-rigged ship proceeding backward at full speed. Now—what was it you wanted to talk to me about?"

"Peter Archer. Just how well do you know him?"

She sat silent and stared straight ahead for some time before answering. "I was his freshman adviser. Why?"

He slowed to avoid a pedestrian and swore under his breath.

"Never a cop around when you need one, is there?" she needled.

He accepted the thrust and smiled. "About Archer," he persisted, "he's missing. According to his roommate, he'd been drinking yesterday afternoon, and came in late with his artificial arm broken. You see where this is leading, don't you, Professor?"

All of her efforts to escape, to evade for a time the fact of Will Gregg's violent death, came suddenly to nought, and she capitulated to its bleak reality. Perhaps she should have known better.

"The classic case of the left-handed killer, I suppose," she said bitterly.

"It's not that simple. As far as we can tell, most of the blows were delivered right-handed."

She made a vague, unplanned gesture of protest. "Well then, it couldn't be Peter—"

"He wears a prosthesis, and it's broken."

"But that's absurd! Worse—it's idiotic! Why, I'm a more likely suspect than Peter—"

"By the way," Jensen said, slowing for a left turn, "where were you between nine and ten last night?"

Her chin lifted slightly, and from the corners of his eyes he could see the set line of her mouth.

"I was home," she said coldly, "writing a magazine article."

"Which brings us back to Peter Archer. He's the only person so far known to have both motive and opportunity."

"That he had opportunity," Natalie began reasonably, "I'll grant you, but that he had reason and *ability*—no. Emphatically no."

Jensen answered with equal detachment. "Motive: he flunked two mid-semester exams, which quite probably cast doubt on his academic future. Now if Doctor Gregg had decided to withdraw his support—"

"He wouldn't!" Natalie broke in.

"Can you prove it?"

"No," she admitted miserably.

"Then we must assume the possibility. My impression of Archer is of a driver—stubborn, strong-willed, and not likely to accept any setback in good grace. Am I right?"

She nodded silently, impressed by his insight.

"I also understand from his roommate that he has a glorious temper, and that he was something less than sober yesterday evening. All in all, it could add up to murder."

"Except that Peter is an amputee."

"Tell me something," Jensen began obliquely, "would you say that Archer thinks on his feet? Is he quick, inventive, seldom at a loss?"

"Yes, but—"

"Then consider the possibility that he struck Doctor Gregg first with his left hand, realized that he'd killed him, and hit him several more times with the weapon in his prosthesis to make it look as if the killer was right-handed."

Concentrating, Natalie brooded in the darkness. "All right," she conceded, "it's possible. A clever man might think of it, with his own life in danger. But aren't you reaching pretty far, Lieutenant?"

"Maybe," he admitted.

"But, as you've said, you have to start someplace."

"Something like that." He sighed. "Frankly, the deeper I get into this case, the less I like it."

"I don't imagine murder is ever a pleasant preoccupation."

"I've worked on cases in which catching a criminal brought its own sort of satisfaction," he said, "but this isn't going to be one of 'em. The cast of characters is all wrong."

"As an historian of sorts"—Natalie, aware of taking on the role of comforter, was wryly amused by it—"I find that the hideous deeds of decent people are not only the most shocking but the best remembered. We're all puritans at heart, I guess."

Jensen smiled, and the shadows on his face shifted to make him look at once troubled and very young. "I hadn't thought of it that way. Thanks."

"I have still another objection to your theory about Peter," she went on. "Even if he did fly off the handle and hit Will, he wouldn't have run away. He'd have called for help. Besides, I don't think he can hold anything securely enough with that hook to strike effectively."

"It can be done, Mrs. Keith," Jensen answered. "That's really why I wanted to talk to you. If you're still willing to help us, I'd like you to witness a test tomorrow at Urban Hospital. I I know this is rough on you, but it would help us—"

"After last night I'm quite immune to pain."

He did not answer at once, but concentrated on parking the car. So he had been right in wondering about this woman and the dead man. He switched off the engine and turned to her.

"The academic world's strange to me, Professor, and it helps to have good liaison. What you're doing is very much appreciated."

"Spare me the patriotic speeches," she said acidly.

"Then I'll make the thanks personal. *I* appreciate it."

"Even when I tell you you're out of your mind?"

"Even if you prove it. Let's go see if we can get a decent meal."

CHAPTER V

At ten o'clock Friday morning Natalie Keith, rubber-jointed with fatigue, pushed her way off a bus and walked the long half block to the main entrance of Urban Hospital. It was a gray day, as yesterday had been, and she was not sure but she thought it was sprinkling snow.

Winter had come, and spring seemed achingly far behind.

The air in the lobby was hot and dry and roared at the people through slatted grills. Natalie pulled off her gloves, stuffed them into her pockets, brushed her wind-disordered hair back from her forehead, and looked about. In front of the information desk was a short line of people, anonymous even in their anxiety, and she joined it. The clerk, her attention divided between the supplicants and a switchboard, seemed to answer as if inspired by some hidden oracle: a prophetess in the Temple of Asclepius.

"Excuse me," Natalie said, "could you tell me—"

"One moment, please." The Servant of the Temple busied herself with a ritual of switches and lights. "Are you registered with the Outpatient Department?"

"Ah—no, but—"

"Well, you should go there first, madam. Come back when you've had a doctor assigned to your case."

"But I'm not a patient," Natalie protested, shaken by the thought of masked and gowned initiates probing her soul and being.

With graceless precision, the Servant of the Temple began sticking plugs into holes in some vague rite of communication. "You're not?"

"No. My name is Keith, and I was told to ask you—"

The Servant of the Temple grabbed a dull red cord and

54

pulled. One plug fell back into its socket with a satisfying thud. "Very sorry, Doctor, I'm sure. I have a message for you." She consulted a note pad. "Mr. Jensen will be delayed, and would you please go to the Rehabilitation Wing on the third floor and wait by the elevators. You'll find benches."

Natalie thanked her, feeling vaguely guilty at pretending to a dignity to which, in this place at least, she was not entitled, and found her way to the Rehabilitation Wing. To her surprise the benches by the elevators were untenanted. In a way she was grateful, although the chance to think in such unexpected privacy made her uneasy. Perhaps, she decided, searching her own defense mechanisms with honest skepticism, she had not wanted to think so much as to daydream. Now she would be able to do neither.

It would be pleasant, she thought suddenly, to own stock in a company that made green paint. There seemed to be a fashion for painting the insides of public places in shades of green ranging from the seasick to the psychological. Urban Hospital had, if nothing else, managed to find a shade even less attractive than that favored by the University.

The thought of the University reminded her of Wednesday night and the hours she had spent alone in her office, thinking. What was the use, she wondered, of staying on? There was every reason for her to leave, both personal and professional. She had gone as far as she could expect in terms of academic rank, and whatever personal joy she might have hoped for had died with Will Gregg. As long as he had been there, everything she did or thought had had both reason and purpose: beyond the pleasure of his companionship, there had been the delight of sharing with him new insights and ideas.

"Speak to the Earth," he had said, quoting Scripture, "and it will teach you." Together they had asked and had been taught, and Will at least had been allowed to touch the fringes of wisdom. It had been he who, gently and lovingly, had shown her that the journey in time from the caves of Lascaux to the stained glass of Chartres was as nothing.

55

> *"Time, like an ever rolling stream*
> *Bears all its sons away.*
> *They fly, forgotten, as the dream*
> *Dies at the opening day. . . ."*

The stream had rolled on, taking Will Gregg with it, and she, remembering the rest of the hymn, found no shelter from the stormy blast, nor any hope of an eternal home.

Three nurses passed in a staccato of white shoes on the dark linoleum. She watched them hurry by down the long corridor and out of sight around a corner. How good it must be to feel that one's life had, ultimately, some value and some worth.

I will leave this place, she thought; I will leave George Durwent and his attendant cherubim and seraphim and never think again of what might have been. Oh Will! I loved you so—

A young woman in a pink smock got off the elevator, leading two children by the hand. Their shared laughter echoed in the hall, startling Natalie and lashing her with sudden irritation. She looked up, thinking wildly that they mocked her, and saw the children's vacant, unlighted faces in brutal contrast to their gaiety. They were blind, and she, shocked and trembling with shame, could only look away.

"It's hard to take sometimes," someone said understandingly.

She looked around to see a young woman in a white uniform and a blue denim work apron. "Especially so," she acknowledged, "if one is busy feeling sorry for oneself."

"I'm Laura Andrews," she introduced herself, "Chris Jensen's friend."

"I'm Natalie Keith." She extended her hand.

"I sometimes feel," Laura said, after a quick inspection of her own fingers, "that I should wear a sign saying 'wet paint.' Chris just called to say he'll be late, and would I take you under my wing until he arrives. I thought you might prefer waiting in the shop to sitting out here."

"Shop?" Natalie asked, totally confused.

"Workshop," Laura explained with a smile. "Didn't Chris tell you what this is all about?"

"Well, he told me you're an occupational therapist, and that I was to be here at ten."

"Oh, good grief—men! He asked me to give a prosthetic demonstration for him and Turk Harrison. You, I gather, are some sort of civilian witness."

"All dreadfully legal, isn't it?" Natalie asked, her voice gone husky.

Laura Andrews looked full into her eyes, the sort of quick, perceptive look that Natalie was not accustomed to meeting in the young. "Chris is a good man, Professor, but he sometimes has an awfully heavy hand."

"Nonsense." Natalie smiled as brightly as she could. "His touch may be ponderous, but my hide is much too thin just now, so it comes out even. I'd be much interested in seeing your workshop, Miss Andrews."

It was a big room, and Natalie's immediate impression was one of well-controlled chaos. Directly before her as she came in was a young woman with badly scarred hands, knotting short lengths of heavy yarn about threads stretched over a frame. Behind her an elderly man worked with great concentration on a floor loom, while a middle-aged woman with severe arthritis labored grimly to shape a lump of clay into a bowl. To her left Natalie saw a young man with a rawhide mallet bandaged to his right hand, working hard to stamp tool a leather belt. Another boy of about the same age, his neck supported in a high plastic collar, was busy doing Palmer Method exercises with a pencil held in his heavily braced right hand.

"Two of our quads," Laura said softly. "One of them broke his neck diving into shallow water, and the other drove a car up a tree."

"Miss Andrews," the man at the loom called before Natalie could speak, "oh, Miss Andrews! I broke a warp thread—I didn't mean to, but—"

"No damage," she answered with a half laugh, "it's easily fixed."

"It is?"

"Sure." Laura opened a small cabinet next to the loom. "All

57

you need is a length of the warp thread and a pin. Then you put in some bridgework—just like a dentist."

Intrigued, Natalie moved closer. In doing so, she bumped the chair of the arthritic potter and apologized.

"That's all right," the woman assured her, "you get used to this madhouse after a while. You should see it when the kids are in—whiz, bang—"

Laura laughed. "Mrs. Collins is our best friend, Doctor Keith, and our severest critic."

"Oh sure," Mrs. Collins snorted, "especially the latter. Tell me, Doctor, are you early for next week's tour, or did you miss yesterday's thundering herd?"

"I'm not a medical doctor," Natalie said.

Mrs. Collins blinked slowly and studied her. "Well, at least you admit it. What are you, a head shrinker?"

"No." Natalie snatched the initiative. "I'm an archaeologist. Did you know your bowl has a distinctly Sumerian quality to it?"

"Sumerian?" Mrs. Collins marveled. "You mean like the Good Sumerian in the Bible?"

"Well," Natalie fumbled, "not exactly—"

She was suddenly and acutely aware that the young woman with the scarred hands was staring at her through the upright strands of her work. To end her own discomfort, Natalie turned and smiled. "I know what that is, Turkish knotting. I've seen it done out East. Are you making a rug?"

The patient shrugged and casually lowered her hands until they were hidden behind her work. "I don't know," she answered, "someone else started this. I'm just doing it to loosen my fingers."

Mercifully, Laura Andrews finished her work and came to the rescue. "This is Miss Finny's first day with us."

"What did you say your name was?" Miss Finny demanded, nothing daunted.

"Keith, Natalie Keith. I'm at the University."

"Oh yeah—I remember. I saw your picture in the paper last night. You're mixed up in that murder, aren't you?"

"Oh *there* you are, Miss Patton." Laura's voice was louder

58

than expected. "I'd like you to meet Miss Finny. She's going to be your patient, so after you've done the evaluation you might start her on a project of her own—"

Miss Patton, wearing a familiar expression of confused willingness, hurried over and took charge of Miss Finny. Gratefully Natalie turned her attention to the rest of the room.

Closest to her was a high, many-drawered bench at which an intent young man in goggles was working with what looked like a dentist's drill. Nearby another equally intent and begoggled patient worked at a small jeweler's lathe fastened to a board that rested on the arms of his wheel chair. The subdued sounds of their equipment were lost in the swamp of louder noise coming from the far end of the room where two men, one on crutches and the other apparently unscathed, were building something that looked ominously like a model guillotine.

Closer to her than the carpenters, on the opposite side of the room from the two machinists, Natalie saw a therapist standing beside an elderly man in a wheel chair. They seemed to be conversing earnestly until, without warning, the therapist lifted his arm, held it up in front of him, and began to pound vigorously on the forearm. Natalie watched with fascinated attention, unaware that Laura had come up beside her. By now the therapist had stopped beating her patient, had grabbed his thumb, and was busily twisting his wrist.

"Technically," Laura said, "it's known as proprioceptive neuromuscular facilitation. Sometimes we also use ice cubes and paintbrushes."

"Is this science," Natalie asked, "or voodoo?"

"The patient's hemiplegic," Laura explained. "He had a stroke several months ago that paralyzed his right side. What Pat— Miss Hull—is doing is triggering a system of reflexes that produce movement at the wrist and fingers."

"I still say it looks more like witchcraft than medicine."

"Maybe"—Laura smiled—"but white witchcraft, please! Some of these reflexes are incredibly ancient—quadruped or even reptilian in pattern—and the whole thing is based on the theory that the cerebral cortex controls movements, not individual muscles."

59

"Splendid, but does it work?"

Laura shrugged. "We usually get some reaction, sometimes a dramatic one. But we haven't been using the techniques long enough to judge if there's carry-over in purposeful motion."

"Laura," Natalie said, "I have a confession to make. I've always thought of occupational therapy as high-class time killing."

"We still suffer," Laura said with a sigh, "from our old Artsy-Craftsy reputation! Webster's dictionary defines O.T. as, 'Any activity, physical or mental, prescribed and guided to aid recovery from disease or accident."

"What," Natalie demanded, "no footnote?"

The phone rang and Laura went to answer. Natalie turned her attention back to the stroke patient, and saw that he had been set up to sand wood, using a heavy two-handled sanding block. He had fallen asleep, to the despair of his therapist, who caught Natalie's eye and smiled.

"Cute, isn't he?" she asked, coming over.

Not certain how to answer, Natalie agreed.

"He's seventy-two years old," the therapist went on, "and has a vocabulary consisting of 'happy birthday' and 'hello,' which is a great improvement over my other aphasic, who can only curse. Poor man, he gets so embarrassed."

"Dear God," Natalie asked suddenly, "how do you girls stand it? You're too young for this much tragedy."

"The world's full of it," the therapist answered quietly, "but it isn't one big ache, you know. It's the sum of little personal things that happen to people like us."

"Excuse me," Laura said, coming back, "that was Chris. Pat, could we move Mr. Samson? I thought we'd use that end of the shop and be fairly inconspicuous."

"It's time he was going, anyhow," Pat Hull answered. "Did you say you have an amputee coming?"

"I hope I do," Laura said, "but you know outpatients! By the way, Professor, will it bother you to watch? I once had a visitor faint colder than a codfish at the sight of an amputee with his shirt off."

"I'll be fine, Miss Andrews."

60

"Well, well," Pat Hull said suddenly, "if it isn't Sherlock himself—"

Jensen, who had come in quietly, winked at her and kissed Laura unexpectedly on the cheek. The young man at the jeweler's lathe gave an expert wolf whistle, and his colleague with the dental drill laughed. Laura offered a classic back-of-my-hand gesture and turned away, red-faced but grinning.

They're a handsome couple, Natalie thought, trying to appear oblivious; young, probably in love, and both of them so vulnerable to human failing. On second thought, maybe they aren't so vulnerable. They have each other, just as I once had Will—

"I have things set up down here," Laura explained. "Our patient should come in about ten minutes, so perhaps we could start."

"You're the doctor," Turk Harrison said cheerfully.

Laura ignored him with regal completeness and led the way to the carpentry area. As they passed, Mr. Samson woke up and smiled.

"Hello!" he said.

"Hi," Laura answered, stopping by him as if she had nothing else to do but chat, "have a nice nap?"

"Oh?" Mr. Samson feigned surprise. "Oh? Hello!"

"Yes, you," Laura said sternly, "you know it's illegal to sleep on the job."

"Oh," Mr. Samson said and chuckled, "happy birthday!"

"Okay," Laura said, "I'll forgive you this time."

He laughed, then turned curiously to Natalie and the two detectives. "Oh? Oh—who—"

"Do you want to know who the visitors are?" Laura asked. "Go on—say, 'Who are they?'"

"Who," Mr. Samson managed boldly, "are—who—hello."

"No, Mr. Samson. 'W-h-o a-r-e t-h-e-y?'"

"Who say—who—oh, HELLO!"

"These are friends of mine, Mr. Samson," Laura went on. "This is Professor Keith, and Sergeant Harrison and Lieutenant Jensen."

Mr. Samson shook hands solemnly, then pointed to Jensen, saluted, and pantomimed firing a gun.

"Do you mean are we soldiers?" Jensen asked. "No, sir. We're policemen."

Mr. Samson's eyebrows shot upward like two startled sea gulls. He looked at Jensen thoughtfully, then thumbed his nose, turned his wheel chair quickly, and trundled off. Laura smothered a giggle as Natalie had a coughing fit.

"Well," she said, "I guess that told you!"

"And they call him an expressive aphasic," Laura marveled.

"He's expressive, all right," Pat Hull agreed, emerging from convulsions of laughter, "just like Harpo Marx! Anything you need, Laura?"

"I don't think so." She unlocked a wall cabinet. "When Mr. Morris comes, just send him back."

Pat left, and Laura began laying out her equipment. "I have a mock-up arm here. It's not exactly like the one you showed me, Chris, but it's near enough to lecture from."

She put the device on the cable and spread the harness carefully, so that it became suddenly clear how it must work. "As you see, it's so simple that it looks complicated. Actually something like it was made in France in about eighteen-sixty."

Natalie's historical instincts quivered and she looked up in surprise. "For a moment I thought you were going to mention Leonardo da Vinci."

"Not this time, Professor." Laura smiled. "Now—as you see, the harness is basically a figure eight with one end left open. The complete loop goes over the sound shoulder to serve as a source of power and as an anchor. One of the open ends goes over the shoulder on the amputated side to hold the socket on, and the other, the lower one, is attached to the cable."

Jensen looked up from the sketch he was doing. "It'd make more sense if you put it on. Or maybe Mrs. Keith would—"

Natalie nodded and slipped into the harness as she would have put on a coat. Beyond where her right fist was crammed into the plastic socket, there extended a bright metal hook exactly like the one Peter Archer wore to replace his lost hand. She stared at it while Laura adjusted the harness to fit her.

"The only thing we have to worry about now"—Laura gave a final tug to the straps—"is the terminal device. You see how the cable attaches to the harness and passes around the outside of the upper arm and down the back of the forearm. The lever to which it attaches there, on the terminal device, is called the thumb, and when it's pulled back—like this—the hook opens. Now—would you reach forward, please, Professor?"

Natalie reached, feeling the harness loop tighten around her left shoulder and the cable pull taut across her back. The hook opened a good two inches.

"Relax."

Again she obeyed, and the hook snapped shut as the harness and cable eased off. Curious, she bent her elbow and studied the hook more closely.

"It's called a voluntary opening hook," Laura continued, "because you have to work to open it. It's closed automatically by these rubber bands, here, at the base of the hook. Each one gives about two pounds of prehension. It's a very simple mechanism, and according to one school of thought, therefore the best."

"Exactly what makes it open?" Jensen asked.

"Look." Laura turned Natalie around. "When the professor reaches forward, her back gets wider. This makes the cable taut, and pulls the hook open. Understand?"

Jensen grunted. "But if widening the back opens the hook, how can you hold anything in the hook and reach forward?"

"Or hit anyone?" Natalie asked grimly.

"By holding the shoulders retracted," Laura answered, "and using trunk rotation instead of shoulder protraction. I suspect each amputee works out his own tricks. As for holding things, the hook can be turned to any position."

Mr. Morris, the outpatient, arrived before she could say more, was introduced to his audience, and proceeded to strip to the waist and put on his prosthesis. He was a stocky man, rather shorter than Peter Archer, but like him had the powerful shoulders of a man who has labored with his body most of his life. Watching him and comparing him to the missing student, Natalie Keith began to feel trapped by the circumstantial evidence that Jensen was so patiently compiling.

"How many rubber bands now, Mr. Morris?" Laura asked.

"Four," he replied. "I tried five, but it made my stump hurt."

"Time, Mr. Morris"—Laura smiled—"give yourself time! Most people never get beyond two or three."

"How many on the arm I showed you?" Jensen asked.

"Four," she answered, "just like Mr. Morris's."

"Is that enough to hold a hammer?" Natalie asked, playing the devil's advocate with a will.

"A light one," Laura answered, almost regretfully, "like this little ball peen. It weighs about a pound, maybe more."

Jensen took it and hefted it, then handed it to Turk Harrison.

"Can you tell me what this is all about?" Mr. Morris asked meekly.

"It's high time we did, sir," Jensen said, with the same deferential, almost shy charm that Natalie had felt so keenly on the night of Will Gregg's death. "I'm a detective with Central Homicide, and I'm trying to find out if a man wearing a prosthesis similar to yours could hit someone hard enough to kill him."

"I can drive nails." Mr. Morris winked at Laura. "But with the other hand it's easier."

"*Touché*, Lieutenant," Natalie said.

He acknowledged her with a wry smile. "There's one thing more, Mr. Morris. If it's necessary—I hope it won't be, but if it is—would you be willing to repeat this test in court?"

Mr. Morris looked straight at him. "I got a son in law school, Lieutenant, and he's all the time telling me about a citizen's duty. Sure I'm willing."

"Thanks," Jensen said. "All right, Miss Andrews."

Laura, who had just put a length of pine two-by-four upright in a vise, took the hammer back from Jensen and held it out to her patient.

"Turn the hook over, please, Mr. Morris, so that the tips point upward—that's right. Now—take the hammer so that the handle passes behind the thumb lever and lies parallel to the back of your arm."

"Like this?"

"Perfect. See that, Lieutenant? A good, strong grip with three points of contact. In fact, a perfect third-class lever."

Natalie, whose knowledge of mechanics was more empirical than theoretical, tried to remember the classes of levers, failed, and resolved to check as soon as possible.

"Now, Mr. Morris," Laura went on, "stand here, just to the left of the timber. Is that right, Lieutenant?"

"Looks good—"

"Okay." She smiled. "Let 'er rip, Mr. Morris!"

He obliged, putting the full power of his shoulder and back into the stroke. The hammer hit with a thud that turned Natalie's stomach and drained the strength from her knees. For one horrible moment she could see the head of a hammer crashing down on Will Gregg's skull, and the fact of his murder, of his violent and needless death, burned itself into and through her consciousness. She could never again think of him without seeing the arc of the hammer descending.

"See?" Laura asked. "The hammer slipped, but it didn't fall out of the hook."

Jensen nodded, and turned to look at the two-by-four. He stood next to it for a moment, running his hands thoughtfully, almost searchingly over its surface. Natalie, watching, wondered if his expression were one of preoccupation or of disappointment. It was, she decided, impossible ever to be sure what this young man was thinking.

It was Mr. Morris who broke the short but pervasive silence. "Find what you wanted, Officer?"

"I think so"—Jensen smiled quickly and brilliantly—"thanks to you! Sergeant Harrison will write out a short statement for you to read and sign, and then we'd appreciate it if you said as little as possible about this to others. After all, no one wants to try a man for murder by means of gossip."

Impressed, Mr. Morris nodded and went with Harrison.

"I'll need statements from you and Laura too, Mrs. Keith," he said, "but they can wait until after lunch."

Natalie, who had taken off the mock-up arm and was nursing a scraped knuckle, looked up in surprise. "What do you do, collect statements as a hobby?"

She had intended the remark as banter, but it sounded harsh and ill-tempered. Startled, Jensen looked at her.

65

"Sorry," she apologized, feeling her control slip a notch, "I'm a little edgy today. Lack of sleep, I guess."

He smiled; not the automatic, professional smile he had given to Mr. Morris, but rather one compounded of humor, understanding, and forbearance. "On second thought, it's too early for Laura to get away, so why don't you and I eat, and then I'll take you home."

The idea of home was suddenly and irresistibly attractive, and she told him so. He agreed, gathered her coat and scarf and, almost without her being aware of it, steered her gently but firmly out of the clinic, down the elevator, and to his car. Only after they had driven half the distance to her apartment did she rouse herself to speak again.

"I suppose that now you'll arrest Peter—"

"When I find him, yes."

"Lieutenant, was that blow really hard enough to kill a grown man?"

They stopped for a light, and he turned to her. "It made a dent almost one eighth of an inch deep in the plank, which would be enough force to break human skin and produce the sort of wounds Doctor Gregg suffered. As to fracturing the skull—as I've said before, I think Archer struck first with his left hand, realized he'd killed, and then switched to the right for camouflage."

"How clever of one of you," Natalie said coldly, "to have thought of that! I wouldn't like your job, Lieutenant. I wouldn't like having the authority to bring a man's life and reputation into jeopardy."

"There are times I don't much like it myself, Mrs. Keith, but my Viking ancestors had a saying—'On law shall the kingdom be built'—and I happen to believe it. Surely you, as an historian—"

"I'm an archaeologist," she interrupted sharply, "I deal in things and places. People are purely incidental."

"I don't believe that," Jensen said gently, "otherwise you wouldn't be so concerned for young Archer—or, for that matter, with Doctor Gregg."

"There *is* such a thing as simple justice, you know."

66

"Yes," he agreed, "except that it's seldom simple."

She was silent a moment. "In all honesty I have to admit that Peter could have done it. But every shred of—well, instinct—in me maintains he didn't. In the first place Will would never withdraw his support of a student for anything short of outright cheating, and Peter didn't cheat."

"I believe you"—Jensen smiled—"the more so since even Dean Durwent had to admit that the boy's honest."

"Millennium!"

"It is remarkable," Jensen agreed, "but considering the evidence we're finding against the boy, your own loyalty is even more so."

"Loyalty!" she burst out. "Is *that* what you think it is? Old school tie—close ranks against the outsiders—"

"We have nothing to indicate that Archer didn't do it."

Natalie's temper collapsed as quickly as it had risen. "I know, and, as you say, he's physically capable of having done it. But it's so improbable—"

"We're working on the industrial-espionage angle," Jensen told her, "but that kind of investigation takes time and tact."

Natalie covered her face with her hands. "It's hard to think of Will involved in anything like that. Oh God, I'm so confused by all this—"

"I don't blame you, and I regret my part in it."

She sat still, staring unseeingly through the window, until they arrived at her apartment building. "I'm afraid I haven't been much help, Lieutenant, nor very good company."

"You've been what circumstances demanded," he answered, stopping the car. "Now go home, eat something hot, and get some sleep. I'll be in touch later."

He came around and opened the door for her, and she smiled uncertainly, offered her hand, and left him without a word.

Upstairs, in her sanctuary, she lay down fully dressed, pulled an afghan over her, and fell at once into a deep sleep. It was dark when she awoke, and she could hear the sound of wind and rain outside. With an effort she roused herself enough to get properly into bed, and slept once more.

67

CHAPTER VI

Saturday morning was gray, and the wispy snow that had fallen during the night was beginning to blow and drift as the wind started up again. It would be gone by nightfall, Natalie Keith reflected as she left her house and went in search of a taxi; the earth was still too warm. At least Will Gregg would not be buried in frozen ground.

There were no taxis, and she decided to walk. It was not far to All Souls Church, and somehow it seemed right and fitting to walk.

There should be mourners, she thought; women clad all in gray and with ashes in their hair, and a procession of offering bearers. So, if we believe history, did Pharaoh go to his tomb. But for you, Will, no wailing, no gifts, no ritual dances—only the unbelieving grief of such as I.

Her way led past a small park where she and Will had often gone to talk or just to sit and watch. Two great Norway maples crowned it, and in the middle of a carefully tended lawn was a large bronze bust of Goethe, his handsome face tear-stained by the rains and snows of fifty years. The past night's wind had torn a small branch from one of the trees, and it balanced like a barbarous wreath above his brow. Leafless and stark; a fitting funeral crown.

Natalie stopped and stood looking at the park. Will had loved this little triangle of earth and grass that stood so stubbornly serene at the convergence of three main roads. Eyes smarting with tears, she turned away: she would not walk there again, for the sight of this small place forced upon her the reality of Will Gregg's death in terms that she could not evade.

All Souls Church became crowded early. Most of those who filled it were of the University, some were friends of Will Gregg from his non-academic life, and others were headline followers. Christopher Jensen was inconspicuous as he waited by the steps, just another serious young man who could be a graduate student, standing and watching. Even Laura Andrews almost walked past before she recognized him.

"Line of duty?" she asked.

He nodded. "I was wondering if you'd be here."

"Oh, us Episcopalians are a clannish lot," she answered. "You might call it line of duty for me too."

"Breakfast afterward?"

"Sure, Chris, but— Well, let's wait until afterward."

"Sorry."

Laura started to say something more, but stopped. "There's Professor Keith. Chris, she looks sick—"

He looked around, saw Natalie start slowly up the steps, and saw a man and woman drift into place beside her. He turned his head, found Turk Harrison in the crowd on the other side of the steps, and nodded. Harrison fell into place behind the lonely woman and her two companions.

When he looked back to Laura, she had gone. Nettled, and also troubled, he started into the church. Laura was nowhere in sight, but Turk Harrison was waiting just inside the doors.

"The man," he reported in a low voice, "is Edward Ken, professor of anthropology. The woman—incidentally, she's Japanese—is his wife."

"Is Mrs. Keith still with them?"

"They've taken her in charge. She looks kind of ill."

"Do you blame her?" Jensen's voice went suddenly bitter. "Turk, I'm beginning to hate this job."

Harrison said nothing, and the first sounds of organ music warned that the service was about to start.

"We'd better go in, I guess," Jensen said.

Natalie Keith, her mind numb and her body moving in obedience to some learning too deep to require thought, heard the priest's words but did not understand. In a voice that seemed to come not from a human throat but from the very fabric of the church, he repeated the promise of One who is both Resurrection and Life, that he who believed, though he were dead, was yet alive. The choir sang, and the crystalline beauty of William Byrd's polyphony reminded her that serenity could still exist, even for her. Will Gregg had died, and so someday would she, but beyond and beneath the mere mortality of humankind was the everlastingness of human creativity. Of the soul and its eternity she had neither knowledge nor intuition, yet suddenly her own experience reminded her that man was more than an organism; that the hearts and minds of men long vanished would have a mortal immortality.

The priest stood, familiar and yet remote in black vestments, and preached of knowing and of doubt, and of the imperfect faith that girds itself with prayer for its own unbelief. Natalie listened, and felt an elusive quietness within her.

"Into Thy hands, Lord," the priest said, and the words were clear in Natalie's understanding, "we commend our brother departed. May the good which he has done, and whatsoever evil he may have had to endure, be unto him for the remission of sin. May he rest in peace, and may light perpetual shine upon him."

He started down from the altar, and Natalie knew that the moment had come when she must admit that the shape beneath the pall was a coffin, and that it held all that remained of Will Gregg. She wanted to cry out in her pain, but the soft moan that escaped her was lost beneath a sudden song of joy:

> "The strife is o'er
> The battle won,
> The victory of life is won;
> The song of triumph is begun
> Alleluia!"

Stunned, Natalie looked toward the choir and beyond at the altar. As its solemn beauty blurred with her tears, she realized that Will's life had been truly a battle and that, for him, its end was in every sense a triumph. The defeated thing in the pall-draped box was not Will Gregg: it never had been.

Christopher Jensen, sitting far to the side of the church, had watched the congregation more intently than he had listened to the priest. On the opposite side of the building he saw Turk Harrison on his knees and realized to his own surprise that they were not so much mourners as avengers; instruments of human law rather than servants of the divine.

He looked away from his more devout colleague and found Natalie Keith. She had appeared ill when she entered the church, but now, though still drawn and exhausted, her look had changed subtly to that of one just emerging on the far side of crisis. Once, as the choir began its final hymn and the clergy started down toward the casket, he had seen her throw back her head as if to cry out, yet she had not. His own men had reported to him that it was possible for someone to enter and leave her apartment building without being seen, and the idea that she might have done just that on the night of the murder stuck in his thoughts like a burr. She was no ordinary mourner at the funeral of a colleague.

Breakfast with Laura did something to restore his spirits, yet in response to her gentle probing he was irksomely unable to explain his own peculiar mood. He had a good suspect in Peter Archer and had begun building a strong case against him, yet there was still something that rankled; something that worked to pry loose the facts he was tucking so neatly into place.

"That's the crux of it," he said with a sigh, crumpling an empty cigarette pack. "As you yourself helped prove, Archer could have done it. My feelings just don't make sense."

"How sad," she said, half mocking, "that men can't have intuition."

"Meaning?"

"That the subconscious is often more perceptive than the conscious mind. I can think of one very obvious reason why Archer couldn't have done it. After all, he's not a *bilateral* amputee—there's nothing wrong with his left arm, is there?"

Jensen, glooming again, shrugged one shoulder. "No, but as Mrs. Keith herself said, he's clever and quick-witted. I figure he struck first with his left hand, killed his man, and then used his right to confuse us. Besides, doesn't some psychologist or

71

other say that under stress a person with shifted dominance tends to revert to his original handedness?"

Startled, Laura blinked and looked at him. "I'm sure," she conceded, "that if you looked long enough, you'd find one who said that—yes."

"Oh damn," Jensen swore softly, "I ought not to be talking to you about this."

"Why not? I'm already involved, and if that's not enough I'm going to marry you. There's no law against detectives' talking to their wives, is there?"

Jensen smiled. "If there is, I'll transfer to the Sanitation Department. Isn't it time the clergy got back from the cemetery?"

"About. Let's go see."

He was silent until they came in sight of the church. Then, as if its unapologetic simplicity forced him to grapple again with his problem, he found himself going back over his misgivings about the case and its principals.

"Laura," he said, "how do you feel about Mrs. Keith?"

"As if I'd like to know her much better. She must be a fascinating person to have for a friend."

"How'd you describe her?"

She considered the question. "She looks rather like Katherine Hepburn, with a dash of Helen Hayes."

"Now that," he groaned, "is a detective's nightmare!"

"Why? Could you do better?"

"Well—no."

"She was in love with Doctor Gregg," Laura asked casually, "wasn't she?"

Jensen stopped in his tracks. "Good grief! Was she? Is *that* what's wrong?"

"What's so wrong about being in love?" Laura asked objectively. "Unless, of course, you're already married to someone else?"

"You don't understand, Laura. She's a suspect—not a very major one, but a suspect."

"Oh, Chris, don't be silly!"

"She wouldn't, given the right amount of pressure, be incapable of murder."

72

"Neither would ninety-nine per cent of the human race, including you."

Jensen fumbled for a cigarette. "At the moment I'm thinking seriously of murdering the dean. *Blast* the old fool! To involve a woman was bad enough, but a woman who loved the victim— if I'd suspected—no, come to think of it, I did suspect—oh damn it all, Laura, do you know what I'm doing to that woman?"

"I have a pretty fair idea, Chris."

"Well, it's going to stop."

"No." Laura put her hand on his. "That would only make it worse for her. She's already in this almost as deep as you and Turk, and to force her out now would leave her nothing to cling to."

"You may be right, but—"

"There's Father Bates," she said, "just going into the church. Ask him about it."

The rector was slightly surprised to see them, but waved them into his office to wait while he took off his vestments. Jensen, still pondering what to do about Natalie Keith, was not at all prepared to begin his questioning when the priest joined them.

"I'm delighted to meet you, Lieutenant"—Father Bates offered a large and surprisingly hard hand—"even though I was somewhat startled when Laura told me she was engaged to marry a policeman."

"Yes, sir." Jensen felt inordinately foolish.

The priest settled himself behind his desk, put his telephone carefully into the top drawer, and closed it. "Out of sight, out of mind," he said pleasantly. "Now—where shall we begin?"

With his second shock of the morning, Jensen realized that the clergyman was prepared to offer them premarital counseling. He made a desperate effort to organize his thoughts, and began to talk.

"Well, sir," he began, "I have some questions—about a crime," he added in panic.

An expression somewhere between relief and caution crossed the priest's face. "Will Gregg?"

"Yes."

Father Bates leaned back and looked at them. "It's a funny thing the way Will's life—and his death—have touched other people. As Mrs. Keith said, the most unique of all the human qualities is man's ability to appreciate the irony of his own situation."

"I'm worried about her, Father," Laura said. "I don't think she should be alone just now. She should be busy——"

"She's being cared for," he answered. "Some friends of hers, a Doctor and Mrs. Ken, have taken charge."

Relieved, Laura nodded. "You and Chris want to talk, so I'll go browse in the library."

"You might go to the rectory," Father Bates suggested, "and inspect my new son. Barbara and I are unbearably proud of him."

"I'll do it." Laura smiled. "Thanks."

"Now," the priest said when he and Jensen were alone, "what may I do for you?"

"You can tell me everything you know about Will Gregg."

The priest stared at his hands for a moment. "I was his spiritual director for ten years, Lieutenant, but what I know about him and what I can tell you are two quite separate things."

Jensen looked up sharply.

"The seal of the confessional."

"For an Episcopal clergyman?"

"It applies to all clergy—Roman Catholic, Presbyterian, Holy Roller, even Episcopal. I believe a rabbi can also claim it."

Jensen's frustration bolted with him. "Damn it, this is a homicide——"

"Believe me, Lieutenant, this is almost as galling to me as it is to you."

"But there must be some way——"

"May I ask a question?"

"Of course."

"If a man lost his birth certificate, could he obtain a copy from the Passport Bureau in Washington?"

With difficulty, Jensen mastered his temper. "I think so," he answered stiffly.

"An annoying thing, bureaucracy," the priest rambled on, "but it has its own peculiar efficiency. It astounds me how much we reveal of ourselves on forms and questionnaires. Future biographers of obscure poets and minor scholars will find Washington a gold mine of trivial and homely details—"

A subtle excitement touched Jensen and spread through him as the clergyman spoke. Passports. Anyone traveling outside the United States needed a passport. South America was definitely outside the United States.

With a slow and thoughtful gesture, Jensen closed his notebook. "I understand your position, Father; I understand perfectly. Thanks for your time, and when we meet again, I promise crime will have nothing to do with it."

"The happier side of a policeman's lot, perhaps?" The priest stood up, smiling. "Laura's a fine young woman, Lieutenant."

"I know it, sir. And thanks again. That's all right, I can find my way from here alone."

Natalie Keith rode in silence between Edward and Michi Ken, rousing only when they stopped before the deceptively stark house in the suburbs. She smiled as warmly as she could and apologized for being dull company.

"You're not company, Nat," Edward Ken said, "you're more nearly family. Isn't she, Michi?"

"Very much so," his wife answered, "and we have no dull relatives. Will you help me in the kitchen, Natalie?"

"If I can, Michi. I'm not much of a cook."

"I am, so it won't matter. I'll teach you Japanese cooking."

"And I," Edward Ken added, fumbling for the door key, "will mix us all an American drink. Or pour saki, if you insist."

"I insist," Michi said severely. "Whisky would numb the tongue."

"My beloved wife"—he opened the door with a flourish— "what do you think saki will do to it? My God, the stuff melts steel—"

"But it goes better with Japanese food," Natalie said. "Honestly, you two, I appreciate this—but don't go to trouble on my account. I'm all right."

Edward Ken took her firmly by the shoulders. "You are with us, and with us you will stay. Let's go into the living room while I build a fire. There's time before malnutrition sets in, and it's a good day for a fire."

The room was beautiful in its uncluttered simplicity, its clear, clean color, and its quiet. In her weariness Natalie yielded to it at once. The physical comfort of a soft chair, the warmth of her friends' concern, and the power of the saki soon stripped her of all reticence. Will Gregg had loved these people, and so suddenly did she: for a time she sat silent, clinging to the kindness and peace that surrounded her.

Edward Ken selected a Mozart symphony and started loading the record player. "Repressing of an old Toscanini," he said casually, "better than any of the new ones, for my money."

"I believe it," Natalie agreed.

He finished and turned on the machine. "How about a refill?" he asked and reached for the decanter.

"I oughtn't—"

"That's a good reason for doing so. Give me your cup."

She obeyed, aware that the thimble-like cup trembled in her hand. "Edward," she asked slowly, hearing her own voice as remote, "what do you know about Will before he came here?"

"Nothing." Ken poured for his wife. "I never asked, and he never told me."

Natalie half smiled, aware that the words might have been meant as a rebuke and, equally, that they were not. "He was that sort of man, wasn't he? But his past bothers the police, Edward. They seem to think there's something sinister about it. Funny, isn't it? To think such a thing about Will—"

"To us, yes, but I can understand how they feel. That Lieutenant Jensen has a reputation for thoroughness."

"He's a nice boy," she said, "quite young, but competent. One could like him if he weren't a policeman."

Ken nodded and said nothing for a moment. "Isn't it possible, Nat," he asked hesitantly, "that he's right about wanting to know more of Will's past? After all, we don't know—the answer may be hidden back there somewhere."

She raised her cup and drank. "I suppose, but I wonder. Is the answer to Will's death there—or to his life?"

Ken raised an eyebrow and looked at her.

"What I mean," she continued, failing to notice that he refilled her cup again, "is rather like what Father Bates said— 'the good which he has done, and whatsoever evil he may have had to endure'—that sort of thing." She paused and drank. *Something* must have made him the kind of man we knew. A child is a neutral sort of creature, after all, and I don't care what Wordsworth had to say about it. It's life that's father to the man— God, am I making any sense at all?"

"You're making all sense, Natalie san," Michi answered.

"In vino veritas." She smiled. "I'm rather drunk, you know."

"As you said"—Ken nodded—"in wine there is truth."

She contemplated her cup, then held it out to be refilled. "Michi san, would you do something for me?"

"If I can—"

"Cut my hair."

Ken turned sharply and looked at her. "My dearest Natalie, you are neither Antigone nor Electra—"

"And Will was neither Oedipus nor Agamemnon, I know." She turned away, avoiding his look. "He was just—he was just Will, and I loved him!"

Michi came and sat on the arm of her chair, not speaking, just providing a presence and a warmth in a world gone empty. Natalie leaned against her and gave up trying to control her hurt.

"He was all I had," she said in her bewilderment, "all I wanted. I loved him, and he's gone. All my life it's been that way—everyone I've ever loved—I wish to hell I could die and get it over with!"

Michi signaled her husband to go, and put her hand on Natalie's shoulder. As if the touch were a release, Natalie began to weep with the hopeless intensity of a child who is alone and lost in a strange place. After a time, more exhausted than relieved, she grew quiet again. Michi eased her back into the chair and gently brushed her hair away from her face.

"I'm sorry," Natalie whispered.

"Natalie san," Michi said, "when I was a small child I was taken to Japan for the funeral of an uncle whom I had never met. It was a Buddhist funeral, very simple and very beautiful, and I will never forget what the priest said. When we lose someone we love, it is true he is no longer physically with us, but because we have loved him something of him remains alive within us. The things that pleased him will now please us because we remember him."

Natalie closed her eyes as the tears started again, but now she wept more quietly. Edward Ken wandered back into the room, carrying a pair of his wife's slippers in one hand and a glass of brandy in the other.

"Here," he said, handing the glass to Natalie, "it may make you sick, but it was made from honest French grapes and it's good for what ails you."

She took it, sniffed mightily, and moistened the tip of her tongue with the brandy. "Wasted on me now."

"Nonsense!" he said. "Now—will you two women *please* feed me? I'm hungry."

"It won't hurt you," Michi answered, "you're getting fat."

"I'm getting no such thing! Natalie, you heard my wife, my very own wife, cast aspersions on me—"

"Well," Natalie hedged, "let's say you're losing your undergraduate contours—"

"Well, I suppose that's what comes of giving women the vote—"

"Oh, Natalie's not siding with me," Michi said brightly, "she's just afraid of what I may do to her hair. Assuming, of course, that she still wants me to cut it."

"The sooner the better," Natalie said.

Edward Ken muttered under his breath and sat down. "All right, you dyed-in-the-wool archaeologist, if you must go into classical mourning, go—but do stop short of shaving off your eyebrows."

Natalie smiled unsteadily. "I don't own a deceased cat, Ed-

78

ward. I don't even like cats. I'd have been a dismal flop in ancient Egypt."

"I doubt it," he said, "and anyhow—short hair might look good on you. All I really ask is—can we eat first?"

Michi Ken stood up and held both hands out to Natalie. "The man of the house has commanded. It is for us to obey."

Natalie started to get up, but sat back heavily. "I seem," she announced with solemnity that ended in a half giggle, "to be somewhat less than sober! Which of my three or four left feet did I trip over?"

"The one in the middle," Ken answered, catching her by the wrists and hoisting her to her feet. "Go with Michi, old girl, and have a good cry over the onions."

"I've already had one," Natalie said, "but if you insist— I really don't know what I've done to deserve friends like you two—"

The women left, Michi with a protective arm about Natalie's waist, and Edward Ken watched with a worried frown darkening his uneven face. In all the years he had known her he had never before seen Natalie Keith adrift. He had seen her relationship with Will Gregg slowly thaw her taut reserve, had seen her bitter wit mellow into lively humor and her interest in her students grow beyond their ability to absorb facts into a concern for them as people. But now, her guide and support gone, he was frightened lest she had completely outgrown her armor and been left vulnerable. If she had, the unknown man who had murdered Will Gregg might claim another victim.

CHAPTER VII

At eleven o'clock on Sunday morning Natalie Keith awoke in her own room and spent the next ten minutes trying to remember exactly how she got there. She remembered the funeral with, if anything, too great clarity, and she remembered that the Kens had taken her home with them. She also remembered having come apart in the shelter of their friendship, having drunk too much, and having become terribly involved in the preparation of a Japanese meal. Obviously they had worn her out with complications.

The saki had helped, she decided, pressing her fingers experimentally against her temples. Then, startled by what she felt, she sat up and stared at her reflection in the mirror across the room: her hair, once shoulder length and worn in a French twist, had been cropped short.

In that moment her vague feelings of strangeness and alienation crystallized about the unfamiliar image in the mirror. Yesterday his fellow creatures had given their final blessing to Will Gregg; today she must start learning to live her own life without him. From now on, each day would add to the separation between them, and perhaps someday, just as she was growing used to the face in the mirror, she would become accustomed to a world and a life in which Will Gregg was a memory.

She got up and went to the kitchen, started water for coffee, and went back to dress. On the hall table she found a note from Edward and Michi Ken, urging her to call them if there was anything she needed or wanted. She read it twice, thinking that such kindness was seldom met, and that perhaps their own aloneness had given them special skill to deal with hers. Perhaps distance had loaned them not enchantment but compassion.

Edward Ken, London-born, but reared and educated in

Chicago, had never relied overmuch on outside opinion. One came to know him slowly, and only as deeply as he allowed. She remembered that he had been Will Gregg's friend before he became hers, and that she had almost failed to share Will's happiness when Edward had suddenly married a Japanese artist who was fifteen years his junior. Now, thinking back, she could see that this man, who lived as his conscience directed, would have married the lovely Michi no matter what his friends thought.

The sudden sound of her doorbell startled Natalie from her thoughts, and she hurried to answer. To her surprise the caller was Laura Andrews.

"Hello," the girl said, "how goes it?"

"I have a hangover, thank you," Natalie answered frankly. "How are you? Come in and have some coffee to thaw out. You look half frozen."

"It's cold," Laura agreed, "but beautiful. In fact it's so beautiful that Chris and I were wondering if you'd go out to dinner with us. He'll be along in a moment. By the way, are you allergic to chrysanthemums?"

"That's very kind of you—really?—and no," Natalie answered. "Now—please come in and tell me what you're talking about."

Laura grinned and offered a florist's bundle. "We're driving into the country to enjoy whatever's left of the foliage and have dinner at a place Chris knows, and we thought it would be fun to have you join us. All very simple and totally selfish on our part."

"Another part of the conspiracy to keep Keith from brooding?"

"Yup." Laura decided that honesty would be more persuasive than diplomacy. "By the way, I like the new hairdo."

"I feel skinned and ventilated." Natalie ran her hand over her head. "Yellow chrysanthemums—they're lovely! Warm as sunlight and lively as spice. Thank you both."

"I wanted heather," Laura confessed, "one Scot to another, and all that, but I couldn't find any."

"I'm only a Scot by marriage, you know. Do you like

81

scrambled eggs? I'm starved. I wonder if it was all that Japanese food—"

"Doctor Keith, it is now *my* turn to ask what *you're* talking about."

"If I knew, Laura, I'd tell you. Be an angel and reach two plates in that cupboard, will you?"

Laura obeyed, and turned to see Natalie deftly breaking eggs into a skillet with one hand. "Hey, where'd you learn that? You're an expert."

"When I was at Mycenae, about a hundred years ago, we had an old Greek sailor for a cook. He taught me this, and a lot of other oddments."

"Do you speak Greek, Mrs. Keith?"

"I used to defend myself." Natalie served the eggs. "Now—off to the living room for breakfast."

"Here"—Laura reached out to take the tray—"let me do something to help."

"Thanks. I'll bring the coffee."

Laura followed her into the living room. "How wonderful to have windows that get the winter sun!"

"It helps. It's an awfully old building, but it has the advantage of large rooms, big windows, and closets. That's why I cling to it, I guess. There wouldn't be room for me and all my books in one of those magazine illustrations."

Laura grinned at her, and Natalie decided that there was no pretense in the girl.

"You sound like an O.T.," Laura said. "As a profession, we're a bunch of pack rats."

"I'm not surprised, considering the range of knowledge you need. Where do you live, Laura?"

"In the nurses' residence at Urban, but I'm looking for a place. I'm getting married soon."

"Lieutenant Jensen?" To Natalie's surprise, the girl blushed. "I wish you all the best, child. When is the happy event?"

"It depends," Laura hedged. "Doctor Keith, may I ask a question?"

"Only if you promise to stop calling me by that pompous title. What's the question?"

82

"Is that a Greek amphora on the shelf by the window?"

"Not quite." Natalie admired the deftness with which Laura had changed the subject. "It's supposed to be Etruscan. Actually I'm not convinced that it's authentic. There've been so many Etruscan forgeries— Look here, would you like to see my collection?"

"I'd love it!"

"Really," Natalie asked, "or are you being polite? I'm quite capable of being a bore, you know—"

"If you hadn't invited me, I'd have asked."

"Finish your eggs," Natalie ordered, "and follow me."

What Will Gregg had dubbed the "Keithsonian Institution" was in the smaller bedroom, and when she entered it Natalie was struck by its similarity to Will's study. It was not so much the furniture—one display case is, after all, much like all others —but in the atmosphere of the place.

And why not? she wondered; the first thing we found we had in common was a tendency to comfort ourselves with the beauty of the past. The rest, finding comfort in each other, came later.

The sight of Laura Andrews staring fascinated at a display of Egyptian small art reminded Natalie that the past was greater than her own memories. She closed her eyes and tried to recall the world beyond her own.

"My best pieces are on loan, though that unguent jar is a nice one."

Laura smiled and pointed to a large limestone chip with a painter's sketch still fresh on its surface. "This sounds crazy, but that face looks familiar."

"You have a good eye," Natalie answered. "That's probably the famous Queen Nefertiti. It comes from 'Amarna."

"You never think of Egyptian art as being so free," Laura mused, "at least, I don't. I always think of people standing around like chiropractor's nightmares."

Natalie laughed, fully and deeply. "That's the best description I've heard yet! But if you've ever done mechanical drawing you'll see that the Egyptian technique is very like orthographic projection. The distant doesn't recede, it gets piled on top of the foreground so you can see the whole picture at once."

Laura shivered. "You make it seem awfully real."

Natalie went to her desk and took her keys. "Look at this." She opened a cabinet and took out the cover of a ceramic jar. "These are the fingerprints of the man who painted this more than twenty-five hundred years ago. I sometimes think our civilization puts too much stress on time, and not enough on continuity."

"Maybe," Laura suggested, "that's why we read so many historical novels."

Natalie snorted, half amused, half in derision. "Possibly, but judging by some I've read, not probably."

Laura laughed and reluctantly gave back the jar lid. "That's an interesting thing," she said, pointing. "It's not Greek, is it?"

"Minoan. Kamares pottery from the first of the late Minoan period. Wonderful design, isn't it? The rhythm of the pattern would carry it even without color."

Slowly the two women moved about the room, stopping to study a fragment of Greek marble, a Roman bronze, or the miniature splendor of a Byzantine ivory crucifix. In the presence of so great antiquity, the small difference in their own ages vanished, and they spoke as friends of things they both admired. The spell persisted even after the last case had been studied and there were only a few photographs on the wall to look at.

"Family." Natalie nodded toward a fading picture in a gilt frame. "My father was a doctor and my mother taught school. The stuffy kid in the boiled collar is my brother, Arthur, a very big man in a small town. We haven't spoken in twenty years."

"You don't look at all alike," Laura observed.

Natalie gave her a look of gratitude. "That's Ben." She stopped before a portrait of a young man in an Army captain's uniform. "He was killed in Africa in forty-three. The rest of these are just snaps with inflated egos, though that's not a bad study of Knossos, if I do say so myself."

Laura paused before a picture of two people standing in front of an old, open cockpit airplane. "Hey," she said, "isn't that—oh, what's her name?—the one who was lost at sea—Amelia Earhart?"

"Right!" Natalie said. "I'm surprised anyone your age would recognize her. You must have been in diapers in nineteen-thirty-seven, when she died."

"Not quite, but thanks anyhow! I think she's a hobby with Chris. If he's described her disappearance to me once, he's done it a dozen times. Who's this standing beside her?"

"Me," Natalie answered quietly.

Laura's jaw dropped. "You *knew* her?"

"Oh Lord, no! This was taken after I'd kept her waiting twenty minutes to land. She was very decent about it, and even admitted to occasional jitters when she was a student pilot. The only other time I ever saw her was a few months later, at a publishers' dinner in New York, just before her last flight. She was married to a publisher, you know."

"I didn't," Laura said, "and please don't tell me more until Chris gets here, or he'll never forgive me."

"There's nothing more to tell."

Laura started to say something, then scowled thoughtfully. "Hold it! Let's back up a ways. If you kept her from landing, and she— Are you a flyer, Mrs. Keith?"

"I have been since I was eighteen. I'll take you up sometime, if you like."

"Golly," Laura said, and it occurred to Natalie that for all her knowledge and human insight she really was quite young.

The extension phone rang brassily and Natalie lunged to pick it up. "Well, Lieutenant, I'd forgotten you! Have you been busily discouraging crime or . . . Oh, looking for a parking place. Well, of course you can't find one! Can one ever? . . . Fine, we'll expect you when we see you."

She hung up and smiled shyly at Laura. "He probably thinks I'm nuts. The truth is, I am slightly manic."

"I'd be worried," Laura answered frankly, "if you weren't showing some sort of reaction."

Natalie turned away, her minor crest of elation draining as quickly as it had risen. "Laura, at this point, I don't know who

85

I am, or where I'm going, or even *if* I'm going. All I'm sure of is that I have better friends than I deserve."

"That's true of everyone, Mrs. Keith."

"I wonder," Natalie answered. "I've never been what might be termed 'popular'—in fact, I have a reputation for being somewhat nettlesome."

"Not absent-minded?"

Natalie smiled, slowly at first and then more freely. "Not yet, but I wonder. I gave two lectures on Thursday, and for the life of me I can't recall if I preached on Socrates to a seminar in field archaeology or taught the kids in History 1 how to dig trial pits."

"Well," Laura said in mock seriousness, "education should be a well-rounded experience."

"Not *that* well-rounded!" Natalie protested. "But in a way I hope I did get scrambled. It'd be fun watching people try to be tactful while asking me what the hell I was talking about."

The doorbell rang and Natalie jumped, betraying her tension. "That'll be your detective. Do the honors, please, Laura, while I put the coffee on again."

"'Scuse me, lady," Jensen said as Laura opened the door, "I'm taking up a collection—"

"Mrs. Keith," Laura called, unperturbed, "where do you keep your trash? There's a man here—"

"Hold it!" Natalie replied, "my neighbors began suspecting I was batty when I had an Egyptian mummy delivered by parcel post. Are you trying to convince them?"

Jensen looked at Laura and raised an eyebrow; in answer, she shrugged one shoulder.

"Chris, did you know Mrs. Keith flies an airplane?"

"Sure," he answered, "she was a ferry pilot during the war."

"Oh nuts!" the girl complained. "I can see where being married to a detective's going to be hard on the ego."

"That's okay, you're a much better carpenter than I am."

"Thanks a bunch!"

"Think nothing of it," he said grandly. "Is that coffee I smell?"

"Warmed over," Natalie answered. "Come into the kitchen and have some. Where'd you park?"

"Out front, in a hack stand. It's wonderful what a badge can accomplish in this democracy."

"I hope you get a ticket," Laura said peevishly.

"I have connections." He stirred his coffee. "Mrs. Keith, could you fly from here to Washington D.C.?"

"It's been done," she answered noncommittally. "Why?"

"Thither the threads of inquiry leadeth," he said, and Laura made a pained face. "Could you take tomorrow and Tuesday off and fly Turk and me down? In an official capacity, of course."

"Theoretically, yes; actually, no. At least not unless your connections are with high places. All flight plans must be filed in advance of take-off."

"They were filed last night," he told her. "I tried to get you on the phone, but you were out."

"I was knee deep in Japanese food, and, I suspect, three sheets over from drinking saki."

"Lethal stuff," he agreed. "Will you fly us?"

"Haven't you forgotten something, Lieutenant?"

"Like what?"

"Like an airplane."

"Oh, that." He smiled. "The city has resources that the simple taxpayer knows not of."

"Presumably including other pilots. Why use me? I want to make the flight, but I'm curious."

"I may need you to identify Doctor Gregg's handwriting."

"We'd better leave about dawn," Natalie said soberly. "By the way, what's the weather forecast?"

"Just like today, beautiful. Now—how about dinner in the country?"

As she changed her clothes, Natalie reflected, that a few hours earlier she would have refused even to consider eating out. Now it seemed not only unavoidable but desirable. These were pleasing young people; wise beyond their years in the ways of humankind, yet buoyant enough to carry their wisdom lightly. In her present state of suspension she found their attraction irresistible.

The place that Jensen had chosen for dinner was a two-hundred-year-old inn, carefully remodeled to serve a less leisurely age. Natalie's professional eye followed the sweep of the old road up to the long, pillared porch and came away satisfied: whoever had done the restoration was a person with a well-nurtured sense of history.

"Is this the place you told me about last spring, Chris?" Laura asked as they followed the hostess to their table.

"Yes. Harry's done a nice job on it."

"He certainly has," Natalie put in. "I'd guess he went through every old barn within a hundred miles to get those beams."

"Oh, he's a perfectionist, is Harry." Jensen grinned. "But he'll appreciate any criticisms from a pro."

"Is he an architect?" Laura asked.

"Darling, you sound so suspicious."

"Well, you have some—ah—*unusual* friends."

"Harry was the best correspondence-school architect State Prison ever had," Jensen said, sounding hurt.

"Mrs. Keith," Laura asked shakily, "would you please ask him why Harry was in State Prison? I'm afraid to."

"He was chief guard," Jensen said with a straight face.

Natalie looked from one to the other and then retired behind her menu. "I've never had a hangover affect me like this," she mused. "Of course, I haven't had very many—"

"One becomes immune after a while, I hope," Laura observed.

A waiter arrived, and while Jensen ordered, Natalie studied the room with its aged beams and hospitable fireplace. It was a curious blend of the modern and the old, and it caught her mood of suspension between two lives and reflected it without mercy, but with grace. That Will Gregg was dead was as undeniable as the truth that she herself still lived and must go on living. The past and the present; indivisible, yet separate.

"Will Gregg would've liked this place," she said aloud. "He was like a child when it came to wanting the 'right setting' for special meals. Last summer we flew all the way to Maine for lobster, which I dislike, in Rockport. But I got my revenge on the way back—we were weathered in at Boston, and I made him eat beans."

"Sadist," Jensen accused.

"Better beans than codfish," Laura said.

"I thought about having a tea party," Natalie added, "but changed my mind."

Laura laughed and told her that she was a good Indian and a sportswoman. They talked on for a time, playing the game of matching meals and settings until the waiter brought their appetizers. Natalie, who had enjoyed the talk, realized suddenly that she had borrowed Will Gregg's favorite means of making pleasant company, and felt her inward tenseness begin to ease. She had never understood before how simple it was to give of oneself to others, and then to step off and let them give of themselves to each other and to her.

The meal was simply served and excellent, and by the time they were finished the afternoon was turning toward evening. They took the long way home, driving in contented silence through an early-winter countryside that seemed a study in gray against a background of deep, cool blue. In the shank of the afternoon they stopped to buy apples and ate them, cool and crisp and juicy, while the sun lowered and the sky turned to dusty purple trimmed with gold.

"Too lovely," Laura sighed as they merged with the highway traffic headed into the city, "too lovely to last."

"Sunday," Jensen said profoundly, "inevitably leads to Monday. Right, Professor?"

"Alas, yes."

"I wouldn't mind so much"—Laura sighed again—"if you got a day off once in a while. This is the first time he's taken in three weeks, Mrs. Keith, and he says he couldn't have taken it."

"Oh dear," Natalie said, "and I was going to ask if you'd come up to my place for a while, and you'd probably rather be alone."

"Where," Laura asked glumly, "in Chris' rooming house, or the nurses' residence at Urban?"

"It's a helluva way to run a romance," Jensen agreed.

"My living room," Natalie said firmly, "is at your disposal. I've got papers to grade, and will be scarce all evening."

Laura turned and looked at her, her expression one of wanting torn by shyness. "That's very kind, Mrs. Keith, but—"

"You'd be doing me a favor, if you must know. For the first time in my life I dread solitude. Just having someone there for a while would help."

"I shall have guilt feelings," Laura said, "but—thanks."

"Me too," Jensen added. "Thank God there's no police regulation against fraternizing with the nice people one meets in the line of duty! We both appreciate it, Mrs. Keith."

"No," she answered seriously, "I'm the one who's grateful. I can't explain it, but just knowing there's someone else there— I'm getting old, I guess, and fretful."

It was ten o'clock when Natalie emerged from her study, tired but relieved at having finally finished grading her term papers. She found Jensen and Laura sitting on the floor, leaning against the couch and listening in silent contentment to Bach's B Minor Mass.

"Hi," Jensen said, "we took you literally and made ourselves homely."

"Good." She linked her hands behind her neck and stretched. "I don't quite see how it's possible, after the meal we had, but I'm hungry. What would you two say to hot biscuits and coffee?"

"We ought to be going." Jensen looked worriedly at his watch. "But—I'd love it."

"Can I help?" Laura asked. "I'm not as bashful as Chris."

"Come out to the kitchen and kibbitz. Maybe you'll help me stay organized."

They followed her to the kitchen where Laura made herself useful and Jensen, forgotten, spotted a paperback book on top of the refrigerator and took it down.

"Taking up anthropology?" Natalie asked.

"Being nosy. 'Ex Libris Peter Archer'—my, my, the plot thickens."

"He left it last Tuesday," Natalie answered calmly. "One of the exams he flunked was mine, but I can assure you that he was in complete control of his emotions. He volunteered to do extra work to raise his mark, and I accepted."

"I'm glad to know that." Jensen closed the book and put it back on the refrigerator. "But it doesn't change the fact that he's our prime suspect."

Natalie leaned against the sink and stared thoughtfully at her hands. "I want Will's murderer caught, Chris, but not at the expense of accusing an innocent man. I think Will would agree that the thing had better go unsolved at that rate."

"You were in love with Doctor Gregg, weren't you?" Jensen asked gently.

She nodded, still leaning against the sink. "We were going to be married this Christmas."

Impulsively, Laura reached out to her. Natalie took her hand and held it for a moment, then stood straight and smiled. "I smell biscuits," she said briskly. "Laura, check the coffee. Christopher—prepare to carry a large, heavy tray."

He obeyed, setting the tray down carefully on the coffee table. "I have a question," he said, turning to attend to the record player. "My theory is that you borrowed the Bernstein record and haven't had time to return it. Laura thinks it was a gift and you're being polite by keeping it."

"And I think you two are a couple of snobs," Natalie answered with a disarming smile. "Bernstein can be very much in the Puccini tradition when he wants to. Someday really listen to the score of 'West Side Story.' This is opera at its lyric Italian best."

"But it's so—so *noisy*," Laura protested.

"I think the same was said about 'Tristan und Isolde' in eighteen-sixty-five."

Jensen, who had been sitting in distracted silence, grunted softly. "She's right, Laura. There is a similarity between 'Un Bel Di' and 'Tonight.'"

Natalie beamed upon him. "Have some more jam."

He accepted. "Laura tells me you have something she wants you to show me—at least, I think that's what she told me."

"The picture," Laura prompted.

"Oh, that," Natalie said. "You can take it off the wall if you like."

"Constant source of amazement, that girl," Jensen said, watching her go. "She's the only person I know who can understand doctors, refinish furniture like an expert, *and* dance."

"Sounds like she'd make a good archaeologist, except for the dancing."

"Who would?" Laura asked, coming back.

"You, oh mysterious one. What have you there?"

She handed Jensen the picture without comment, and grinned when he grunted in surprise and sat bolt upright to study it.

"Are these the people I think they are?" he asked.

"Yes," Natalie answered, "but I assure you, it was the chanciest of chance meetings."

He leaned back, staring at the images of a handsome girl and a tall, slender woman with chaotic hair and an unforgettable, not-quite-beautiful face. "She haunts me. There's something odd about the way she vanished."

"Lots of pilots have been lost at sea," Natalie observed.

"With worldwide publicity?"

"Sure. Take Antoine de Saint-Exupéry, for example."

"Okay, okay," he conceded, "but they didn't even find an oil slick from the Earhart plane."

"Don't tell me you believe that tale about her being taken prisoner by the Japanese—"

"It's not impossible. There's a story about a plane in the shallow water off Saipan—"

"It could be hers," Natalie agreed, "but it's equally possible that it isn't. Mute finds without links to known and dated material exist in limbo. Now if one could get a look at the wreck—"

"If it isn't her plane," Laura asked, "what do you think happened?"

Natalie shrugged. "It's a deep ocean. Actually, I don't think

92

we'll ever know exactly what happened; I'm not even sure it matters. Ours is an age that is starved for heroes, and mystery is, after all, part of the panoply of heroes."

Thoughtful now, Jensen continued to study the picture. "What was she like as a person?"

"Good heavens, Chris, I don't know! I doubt if anyone did, except the few whom she trusted. She never gave up her insistence on privacy. I'll say this, though: when she walked into a room, even if she didn't say a word, you knew she was there."

"I've heard her called egotistical," Laura said, "even arrogant."

"She probably was, on occasion," Natalie answered, "which is not, I grant you, an endearing trait. But 'arrogance' is in some measure a subjective reaction of the spectator, isn't it?"

"Bad public relations on her part?" Jensen asked.

"Sour grapes," Natalie answered. "After all, she wasn't just one professional competing against others. She was a woman contending with, and often outdoing, men in a so-called 'man's field.' Laura's met this attitude, I'm sure. I know I have. It can hurt."

"Oh brother," Laura said, "can't it just!"

"I'd forgotten how long it's been," Jensen said. "I can't think of a thing that hasn't changed since nineteen-thirty-seven."

"And not necessarily for the better," Laura added. "We have a doctor at Urban who maintains that the human race has gone collectively nuts."

"Do you mean Matt Wallace?" Natalie asked. "I don't know how good a doctor he is, but he'd do well professing philosophy."

Startled, Laura looked at her. "How did you ever meet Doctor Wallace?"

"Do you know Doctor Peg Hollander?" Natalie asked. "We were roommates in college, and I'm a chronic guest at assorted medical festivities."

"And what," Jensen inquired, "is the collective diagnosis for our quarter century?"

"The Age of the Prosaic," Natalie answered firmly, "most definitely, the Prosaic."

"How come?"

"No whimsy. No great, irrational flights of poetry. Above all, no heroes. The little, petty, ordinary men have left Odysseus on the beach. We have a dearth of heroes, and a surfeit of heroics."

Jensen continued to look at her, but she sensed that he had retired to the fastness of his own thoughts. It was almost visible, this in-turning, and she envied him the ability to find privacy in the midst of distraction.

"You're right, of course," he mused. "I'd almost forgotten the difference between fantasy and the merely fantastic."

"Pardon me for seeming dense," Laura said, "but just what *is* the difference? I assume it's one of degree, but—"

"If you call a thing or an idea fantastic," Jensen began, "aren't you really saying that it contradicts so-called 'common sense?' But if you speak of fantasy, you suggest something that *transcends* common sense and approaches pure speculation."

"Or pure logic," Natalie offered. "If you accept the premise that there are dragons in the earth, it is quite logical to assume that there will also be Saint George."

"I'd call that symbolism," Laura objected.

"Ah," Natalie said, "but all language, written, spoken, or thought, is symbolic."

"Whoa," Jensen pleaded, "have mercy on a mere cop! How'd we get into this, anyhow?"

"I'm not sure," Natalie replied, "but I think Amelia Earhart's navigation had something to do with it, poor old girl. Do you realize that if she were still alive, she'd be sixty-two years old?"

"Holy smoke," Laura said. "I thought she was in her twenties when she vanished."

"She was a few weeks short of her fortieth birthday," Natalie told her. "As a matter of fact, she didn't become known until she was in her thirties."

"It almost seems, doesn't it," Jensen said, "that we're born to accomplish certain things, and then we die."

"Is that Calvinism," Natalie asked, looking owlish, "Hinduism, or beatnikism speaking?"

To her astonishment, Jensen blushed. "You make me feel

like a beardless kid. After all, your war and mine aren't that far apart."

"Not chronologically," she agreed, "but I'm not so sure of the philosophical distance. I'd like to be around in a thousand years to hear the scholarly debates."

The telephone rang and Natalie uncoiled quickly to answer. "For you, Chris. Laura, let's us make more coffee. This promises to be a long, involved discussion."

It was fifteen minutes before Jensen, looking vague and preoccupied, joined them in the kitchen. "Sorry to tie up your phone so long, Mrs. Keith. That was Turk."

"He didn't strike me as the talkative type."

"We've got Peter Archer," he said after a slight hesitation. "He walked in about an hour ago and gave himself up. So there'll be just the two of us going to Washington tomorrow. Turk'll be busy checking out Archer's story."

"Then he *does* have an explanation—"

"Yeah, he has one"—Jensen ran his hand across his face—"and apparently it's just haphazard enough to be true."

Natalie said nothing, but handed him a cup of coffee.

"Let's just hope Washington proves helpful," Jensen sighed. "God knows, we could use a break."

"You know," Laura said brightly, "I'm not sure I approve of you two toddling off alone together."

"Why not come with us? You and I could do the art galleries while Chris plays detective."

"I wish I could. I haven't been to Washington since I was in high school."

"Was that before or after they shot Lincoln?" Jensen asked.

"You too can be replaced by an IBM machine, Lieutenant!"

"Tell you what," Natalie suggested, "let's plan a flight together. I remember once flying the length of the Shenandoah Valley when the lilacs were in bloom. It was incredible—"

"It's a date," Jensen said with a smile, "but first let's settle the details of this one. Everything's taken care of in Washington, so suppose I pick you up at six tomorrow morning."

"Fine," Natalie said dryly, "but do you suppose I could see the flight plan before take-off?"

"Flight plan?" Jensen looked first blank, then stricken. "M' Gawd! I forgot it—it's right here in my pocket—"

"Darling"—Laura tapped him on the shoulder—"have you ever thought of hiring a secretary?"

He frowned at her, obviously having neither heard nor understood her. "That reminds me, the Duval woman hasn't answered the telegram I sent this morning—"

"Laura," Natalie asked politely, "is it safe to let him out alone?"

"I don't know. Maybe we should call a nice policeman to take him home."

CHAPTER VIII

Natalie was ready early the next morning, arriving downstairs at five minutes to six with suitcase, flight bag, and lunch all neatly packed. She stood by the heavy plate-glass doors, ignoring the curious stares of the janitor and night switchboard operator, and wondered if she had time to go back upstairs for her sunglasses, which she had forgotten.

That's the trouble with five minutes, she thought; it's like a nickel—not good for anything any more. Oh well, I'll buy another pair at the airport. —I hope Edward makes out all right with my classes today. It's awfully short notice—though I must say, Aaron didn't seem surprised when I asked for two days off.

As she thought back on it, Professor Aaron Goldman's calm acceptance of her request began to bother her. It was as if the head of the history department, for all his impeccable Viennese charm, had been waiting for her to come apart at the seams. With the first glimmerings of perspective, Natalie began to wonder uneasily if her instinctive shielding of her relationship to Will Gregg might not be about to backfire.

Anyhow, she thought bleakly, nothing anyone says can hurt Will now. As for me, maybe Lester Tasman had it right when he called me "a tough old bird." Anyhow, if I leave, people will forget soon enough.

At six exactly, Jensen's rain-streaked black Chevy pulled up in front of the building. She gathered her luggage and went to meet him, commenting to herself that he was unusually punctual.

He was not, however, particularly talkative, and Natalie settled down to relax physically while her mind reviewed the flight plan and its alternatives. The weather report had been as near perfect as possible at this season, and it looked as if they would have a smooth flight all the way. Tomorrow, coming home, might be different if the low moved in from the west, but even then it wouldn't be too bad.

"You awake?" Jensen asked.

"Eh-huh. Just loafing while you work."

"We'll be at the airport in about a minute."

She sat up and looked around. "So we will. Do you know where the city keeps its airplane?"

"It'll be parked right in front of the administration building. It's bright green with yellow letters."

Natalie laughed. "Sounds like a taxicab. Do you know what make of plane it is?"

"Nope." He turned into the parking lot. "Some kind of Indian, I think."

"It's always nice to know what you're supposed to fly," she commented wryly. "I do hope it doesn't have feathers on its wings."

He laughed.

"Have you ever flown before, Chris?"

"Once, only I was colder than a mackerel at the time. I was air-evacked from Korea to Japan."

"Sorry. I didn't mean to prod a sore spot."

"You didn't. I was an early casualty, and damned glad of it. I was a pretty lousy soldier until they stuck me in the MPs."

"Once a cop, always a cop."

He turned off the ignition and set the emergency brake. "I wonder," he said gloomily. "Frankly, this case has me jibbering."

With an effort Natalie kept a blank face. "And who," she asked, "are you to be different?"

He smiled, as if to do so was to banish depression. "Now what?"

"Go find your flying Indian and meet me there. I've got to check the weather report and buy some sunglasses. I forgot 'em, like a complete idiot."

He left, carrying her bags and his own, and Natalie hurried into the airport's undersized administration building. The latest weather report remained excellent, and not until she stood waiting to buy her sunglasses did it occur to her that Jensen might have been admitting doubt of his own theory that Peter Archer had killed Will Gregg. She considered the possibility and found it somehow reassuring: no man is more thorough than he who doubts his own inspiration.

She got her glasses and her change and turned to find herself confronted by two men, one of whom carried a large camera.

"Excuse me, ma'am," his companion began, "we're from the *Morning Herald.*"

"A perfectly honorable employment," she said. "Don't apologize."

Startled, the man hesitated and Natalie started to edge past him.

"We'd like a statement," the photographer said quickly. "You are Professor Keats, aren't you?"

"No," she answered, without breaking stride.

"Are you *sure?*" the first man asked, falling into step beside her.

"Young man, is the earth flat?"

"Well, no, but—"

"And my name is not Keats. —Good heavens! Isn't that the governor over there?"

Both newsmen turned, and Natalie kept on walking until she was out of the building. She spotted the green and yellow airplane with Jensen sitting inside and hurried across the chill concrete toward it.

"Hi!" Jensen greeted her, "how did you evade the fourth estate?"

"One of them asked if my name were Keats." She closed the door and reached for the radio headphones. "It isn't, so I just walked away."

Jensen began to laugh and kept on until he realized suddenly that the plane was moving. "Hey," he said, sitting straight, "where're we going?"

"Washington," she answered laconically, and lapsed into the preoccupied silence of one who listens to voices only she can hear.

Jensen gave her an uneasy glance and licked his lips nervously as they reached the end of the runway and turned into the wind. The concrete strip was long and wide, and the plane seemed intolerably small out in the middle of it.

"Clearance received and acknowledged," she said into the microphone, "over and out."

"Y'know," Jensen said, "I think I'll take a train—"

"Shut up!" Natalie ordered with fierce gaiety, doing things that brought the engine's placid throb to full crescendo, "and fasten that seat belt."

Washington was not as its best in the tag ends of autumn. The day was clear and not too cold, as far as Natalie, who was used to a more northerly climate, could tell, yet the land itself looked bleak and dreary. The few leaves still on the trees seemed bewildered to be there, and clung with depressing tenacity. The people of the city, too, seemed uncertain whether to appear in the guise of winter or of fall; few, if any, looked wholly comfortable. She felt curiously superior to the chilly natives when, after checking into the hotel, she left Jensen and started out for the Smithsonian.

It had not changed, and Natalie was dismayed to recall how many years had gone by since the last time she had walked its leisurely, seemingly haphazard aisles. She and Ben had met there for a few hours just before he shipped out; he with a forty-eight-hour pass, and she, by pure luck, with twelve hours to kill before picking up a plane bound for California. They had met under Lindbergh's *Spirit of St. Louis* and spent the morning—it had been miserably cold and wet, she recalled—roaming aimlessly. Then they had parted; each to do what he could, each to pay what was demanded. It had been the last time she had seen him alive.

Now, in the quiet and solitude of the museum, Natalie wondered what her life would have been if Ben had lived to come home. It was certain she would not be here now, the scar of a new hurt still raw, helping a policeman untangle a murder.

Well, she thought, still under the spell of that other day, one does what one can, and pays what is demanded. Perhaps there is nothing more to life than that. Ben paid with his dying, and I—in the classic way of women—paid in grief. It becomes tragedy only if the thing purchased is ultimately of no value. And who but the god you claim you don't believe in can be the judge of that?

She wandered, aware but unseeing, through one section after another, and the ghosts walked with her. First in sadness, then in the pain of loneliness, and finally in the peace of recognition that what was could not be changed for all her yearning, she passed the morning and the early afternoon hours.

Ben and Will Gregg were both dead, and she, for no cause known to her, still lived. With the fatalism natural to flyers and seamen, she knew this to be true only because the time had not yet come for her dying. When it did, she would die and nothing could prevent it, but until then she had no choice but to go on, no matter how lonely or how hurt she was.

At two-thirty, tired and rapidly becoming depressed, she left and took a taxi to the Congressional Library in the somewhat forlorn hope of tracing down an obscure reference alleged to originate in a footnote in a novel by Karl Ebers. That she failed to find it was to no one's discredit, and she left cherishing the idea of giving the task to some hapless graduate student in search of a project for a masters thesis.

She got back to the hotel just in time to meet Jensen for dinner. Since the flight to Washington had first been discussed she had restrained herself from asking him what he hoped to find, but now, confronted by the young man in a distracted, pensive mood, she gave up and asked bluntly for an explanation.

"I came to find Wilson Gregg," he told her, "to learn everything I could about him before he appeared at the University."

"And did you?"

"Yes." He sounded curiously weary. "I found him." He paused while the waiter gave them menus and filled their glasses. "The only thing is—I'm not too sure it helps."

Natalie looked up and smiled as she always did at a student whose knowledge teaches him nothing. Jensen accepted the wordless comment and, after a moment's deliberation, opened his notebook and handed it to her.

"The subject," she read silently, "had top-secret clearance

101

from the FBI. As recently as six months ago he is known to have been working for the Atomic Energy Commission."

"Dear heaven!" she gasped.

"You didn't know?"

"How could I? Chris, so help me, I never knew he had connections with the government. This is fantastic!— Good Lord, do you suppose—"

"That part of the investigation," he answered, taking the notebook back from her, "is in more important hands than mine. I can't afford—at least at this stage—to put too much emphasis on it, but neither can I ignore the possibility that— well, you know."

Yes, she thought, I know. The whole thing could turn into a cheap thriller with Their Men and Our Men lurking in every alley. A surfeit of heroics with no real hero—

"Sticking closer to home, can you identify this?"

He handed her a photostatic copy of a document that she took almost eagerly and spread on the linen before her.

"It's Will's signature, if that's what you mean. Wait—what is this, a passport application?"

"Something of the sort. Look at the date."

"Nineteen-thirty-four— Chris, I don't understand—"

"It's not a pretty story, Mrs. Keith," Jensen said with the resigned air of one used to telling people unpleasant things about their loved ones, "in fact, it's damned ugly. The only bright spot in it is Doctor Gregg himself."

The waiter returned and Jensen ordered. Natalie waited, grimly determined that she would lose neither her self-control nor her temper, no matter what he said.

"At the time that document was filed," Jensen began, leaning across the table toward her and lowering his voice, "Doctor Gregg was employed by a small mining company. He spent about a year in South America looking for mineral deposits and doing such a good job that he was made a partner. Unfortunately the government of the country he was in just then suddenly produced evidence that the company was a fraud. As the only official within reach, Doctor Gregg was arrested and jailed."

102

He paused and looked quickly at Natalie, whose face showed nothing. "The trial, I gather, was a farce. Gregg, who knew absolutely nothing about the company's management, was convicted and sentenced to fifteen years in prison. The embassy—incidentally, they've been very co-operative—has promised to send me transcripts of the trial and newspaper clippings. But there's no reason why any of this should ever be made public."

"Thanks, Chris."

He smiled briefly. "Anyhow, to make a long story clearer, Doctor Gregg served six months—which is where he got TB—and then a native named Hernandes turned up in a hospital badly hurt and made a full confession of his own part in the swindle, clearing Doctor Gregg completely. He was exonerated and became a local hero. Hernandes died, and Doctor Gregg informally adopted his daughter."

"There was something of Don Quixote about him," Natalie said gently.

"I believe it. In nineteen-forty-six, after supporting the girl for years, he sponsored her application for immigration to the States."

"You mean she's here, in this country? Where?"

"I don't know. She entered from Mexico, lived briefly in Texas, and then vanished. For all I know, she's dead."

"How in the name of Pallas Athena did you learn all this?"

"Good luck, plus plenty of expert help."

The waiter reappeared, and for several minutes they spoke of trivialities. Natalie studied the rainbow on the tablecloth where the light shone through her water glass, and wondered about Will Gregg. It was like him to hide not only the ill he had suffered but the good he had done.

"Well, anyhow"—Jensen mustered a smile—"at least I proved that Doctor Gregg was born in Philadelphia."

Natalie smiled back at him, somehow relieved and pleased that his day's research, like her own, had produced little of practical use. The mystery of Will's lost years had been opened, and all that was revealed was that the man's shadow was, if anything, longer and straighter than either she or Jensen had suspected.

"I wonder how Turk's making out," Jensen asked idly.

"You'll pardon me if I don't comment. I wish him well, but I think he's chasing his tail."

Jensen looked up at her. "If he catches it, will I be the one to say ouch?"

"You might. Peter didn't kill Will. Students don't murder professors because they flunk an exam or two."

"Turk was telling me just the other day about a case in which a thirteen-year-old boy shot his mother to death because she wouldn't let him watch TV."

Natalie said nothing, but felt her strength begin to leak away. "Please, Chris. Leave me something to hold on to."

"Oh damn! I'm sorry, Natalie—I mean, Mrs. Keith."

"You were right the first time, and I'm the one who should apologize. Homo sapiens can be the finest of creatures or the most depraved, and I know it as well as you. Only I loved Will, and I'm fond of Peter, and—" She sighed. "Oh, what's the use?"

"Want to know what I think? I think we've both had it for today. How about a quick movie before we turn in?"

"Thanks, Chris, but I'm afraid I'm too tired. It's been an emotionally beating day in its subtle way. I'll see you in the lobby at six tomorrow."

Tired, but too restless to let go of wakefulness, Natalie lay in bed and for the better part of an hour courted sleep. Then she gave up, rose without turning on the light, and went to stand by the window.

Across the city the lighted dome of the Capitol stood out against the sky, reminding her of the Pyramids of Gizeh the last time she had seen them floodlit in the summer dark. She had been in Egypt on sabbatical, ostensibly working on a study of the Osiris myths, but actually running away from a friendship that was growing into love. She wondered if she would be standing here now if five years ago she had turned her back on Will Gregg.

Osiris died in autumn, she thought, snatching a line of half-remembered poetry; he died by violence, and his woman sought his shattered body in the barren places. Will was murdered on the night of first frost, and here am I, in a strange city among

104

strangers, searching like Isis. Oh God, oh God, life takes some bitter turnings!

She reached out, found her cigarettes on the writing table, and lit one. For a moment the glare of the match dimmed the floodlit dome across the city. She sat on the edge of the table and considered the street lights, the headlights of the traffic, and the lights of office windows that burned as fretful symbols of a world's anxiety. A barren place indeed, where peace was not, and where the living sought the dead.

It had been an incredible day, lived in an unbelievable context. A month ago, if anyone had suggested to her that the man she loved was not only an ex-convict but also deeply involved in secret defense work, she would either have laughed in his face or slapped it. The idea of quiet, gentle-humored Will Gregg dodging down back alleys to meet some fellow agent was somehow absurd. Yet it was true, and quite likely the reason why he had died so mysteriously. Killed in action, just as Ben had been.

She stubbed out her half-smoked cigarette and kept on grinding it into the ashtray until it fell to shreds under her fingers. Wraithlike, the intuition of violence presented itself, and was at once repressed.

Remembering Will, she found it less bewildering that he had been the dupe of swindlers. It was altogether in keeping with a nature that could not impute willful dishonesty to any fellow creature. What stirred her was not that he should have gone innocent to prison, but that he should come out and open his heart to a child who had no claim at all to his generosity. He had always seen things as from a height, and now she was not sure if it were Olympus or the Mount of Olives.

He never told me of those years, she thought, appalled to find that she resented it; didn't he trust me, I wonder? Love and trust don't always merge.

Uneasy now, she lit another cigarette and accused herself of behaving like a featherbrained female. There were, she reminded herself, things about her own life that she had never told Will.

Yet she would have told him, had he asked. Of that she was certain. If it was not distrust that kept him silent, what then?

105

Not shame, surely. Plenty of innocent men had been in prison. Sir Thomas More, for one.

The name of the sainted knight brought her thoughts to an abrupt halt: could Will's silence, she wondered, have been due not to the shame he had suffered but to the good that he had made to answer it? Had he been that devout in his belief?

Shaken, and willing to admit that she did not wish to probe deeper, Natalie ground out her cigarette and went back to bed. She had a flight of several hours to make tomorrow, and above all else she needed sleep.

The weather held for the trip home, though it was starting to close in as they neared the municipal airport. Two sleek National Guard jets had landed just before them, and one of the pilots called out to her as she and Jensen started from the hangar to the administration building.

"Still flying windmills, Nat?" he asked.

"Sure," she answered, "I like the little fan up front. It's nice company. How're Marge and the twins?"

"Swell!" He grinned. "When are you coming over for pizza and a little hangar flying?— Oh, by the way, do you know Major Muller?"

"Professor?" the youthful major said, staring thoughtfully at her. "Don't tell me a lady like yourself teaches flying?"

"If you mean me," Jensen said, "I am definitely *not* a student pilot! Natalie tricked me into holding the tiller, or whatever you call it, and I am most surely not the birdman type—"

"He's a policeman," Natalie explained. "I'm an archaeologist."

"Really?" Major Muller asked. "Just the other day I was talking to a BOAC pilot who was in the RAF during the war. He told me about reconnaissance pictures he'd taken over Italy that showed all kinds of ancient roads and ruins. Sounds crazy —how can stuff buried yards underground show up in a picture?"

"There are several reasons, Major," Natalie said, "but it'd take too long to explain them now. I can give you the titles of some books, if you're really interested."

"I got a better idea," the first pilot said, "have dinner with us —you and the policeman both."

"I'd love it, Al, but I'm bushed. But the next time the major is here, call me and we'll celebrate. As a matter of fact, I have some aerial-survey pictures I took myself—"

"It's a date," Muller said, "and soon!"

"Good." Natalie extended her hand. "Al knows how to reach me at home or at the University. Until then, see that you walk away from all of 'em."

They shook hands all around, and Natalie and Jensen went on toward the administration building.

"Natalie," he said as they started for the parking lot, "how do you do it?"

"Do what?"

"Live so comfortably in two worlds. You're as much at home here as you are on campus, aren't you?"

"In some ways, maybe more so. But you should see me on a dig—I'm really a sandhog at heart."

Jensen laughed and fumbled in his pocket for his car keys. "For a moment I was wondering if I'd have to ask you if you also know how to jump ignitions. Laura says my always forgetting car keys has great psychological importance."

"Laura," Natalie grunted, "is a nut."

"Madam, you speak of the woman I love!"

"Well"—Natalie looked searchingly at him—"you're a little east by northwest yourself! I'm sorry this trip didn't turn out better, Chris."

"It was useful." He started the car and backed neatly out of the parking lot. "If you discount that part about the Atomic Energy Commission. Except for that, we clarified some things."

"Can you discount it, Chris? Couldn't it be important, after all? It would be such a wonderful way out—"

"It's not impossible, Natalie, but the consensus was that it's improbable. The Feds are checking it out, and they'll keep us informed."

"Yes," she said glumly. "Meanwhile the setting of our little stage is unchanged. Call me tomorrow, will you?"

"Sure. What's the best time?"

"Being as how it'll be Wednesday, I'd say between eleven and noon. I may be hiding in the broom closet by then, but try anyhow."

"Which one?"

"Which what?"

"Boy, there's a rare bit of syntax! Which broom closet? I don't want to get the janitor by mistake."

Natalie regarded him thoughtfully. "Oh dear, I wonder what'll happen when you and Laura have children. . . ."

CHAPTER IX

It came over Natalie as she entered her office the next morning that it had been a week since Will Gregg died. Seven days, and the placid, timeless existence that is the academic life had smoothed out and resumed its flow as if nothing had ever disturbed it. The flowers on Will's grave had scarcely withered, and already someone else taught his classes and occupied his desk.

Continuity, she thought; impersonal, anonymous, but efficient. The old Arab proverb doesn't hold as far as a university is concerned. They do die who give their lives to learning.

She eased open the middle drawer of her desk and saw the Minoan seal still where she had left it. Gently she touched it with her forefinger, reminding herself that the meanings of past and present are inextricably bound together. Either without the other is valueless.

Twice she had loved and twice grieved, but the first time she had denied that grief, like joy, is common to all humanity. She had mourned Ben alone and forgotten that others too have sadness; had closed her heart and lived only in the awareness of her personal loss. In this sense she had failed Ben and made futile the love he had given her. She must not repeat the tragic pattern with Will.

Her first class, Pre-Classical Civilizations, went smoothly, and for once no one seemed unduly dismayed by her statement that Cleopatra was pure Greek without a drop of Egyptian blood in her. Past years had taught her to expect at least one minor crisis of faith when this was announced, and in a way she was deflated by the docility with which dogma was swept away. Times were changing.

Or else she was.

It was a new idea, and she teased at it as she walked back to her office. Had she changed? And if so, how?

"Professor Keith," someone said, "excuse me, but—"

Startled, Natalie stopped and caught her breath. "Oh, Miss Harper—sorry, I was woolgathering. Is something wrong?"

"Well"—the student smiled ruefully—"yes. About that paper I owe you—"

Natalie considered the girl and frowned. "See here," she said severely, "are you ill? You look terrible."

"I'm all right," the girl protested unsteadily, "honest. It's just —everything's happening all at once."

"Come to my office"—Natalie took the girl's arm—"and talk to me. If you're having trouble, we'll find a way around it. What time did you get to bed last night?"

"I dunno. I didn't notice."

Natalie's frown deepened as she began to recall things about this particular student. She steered her into the office and waved her to a chair.

"Now then," she began, "how many points are you carrying this semester, Miss Harper?"

"Fifteen. But I had eighteen last spring."

"And held a solid B average, if I'm not mistaken"—Natalie smiled—"which is pretty good in my book. You're a junior now, aren't you?"

"Yes."

"And your parents are getting a divorce—"

"What of it?" the girl snapped. "Lots of people do! There's nothing wrong with—with two people getting a divorce."

Natalie got up and closed the door. "Of course there isn't, Linda, except what it's doing to you."

The girl said nothing but bent forward, covered her face with her hands, and wept. Natalie stood where she was, leaning against the door, until she grew quieter.

"You can't run from grief, Linda, because the harder you try, the closer it follows. Believe me, I know—I've tried."

The girl looked up, and Natalie felt her hurt and bewilderment as part of her own. She came and took her in her arms. "It's all right, Linda, it's all right—"

What *am* I doing? she wondered; am I going soft in my old age? I never used to get involved in students' private problems.

110

I've always told Will it's foolish and doesn't— Oh Lord, Will! He always did this sort of thing, and now I'm starting. The trouble is, all of a sudden it seems to matter—someone has to care about this lonely child. I suppose it might as well be me. I don't see George Durwent giving a tinker's dam.

"I don't know what to do," the girl sobbed, "everyone's talking about going home for Thanksgiving, and— Oh, Mrs. Keith, what am I going to do?"

"You'll come home with me," Natalie told her, concluding that she had lost her mind completely, "but that's a whole month off. Right now you've got to start taking care of yourself. What's gone wrong between your parents is no fault of yours, Linda, and tearing your heart out won't help them at all."

"I know, but nothing like this has ever happened to me before, and I'm scared."

Natalie put her hand on the girl's forehead and found it hot and dry to the touch. "I wasn't much older than you—twenty-three, to be exact—when my husband was killed in the war. It's not easy to be left alone without warning. Of course you're frightened, Linda—so was I. But one survives. You really have no alternative, you know."

The girl leaned against her, trembling as much with exhaustion as with emotion. "I'm sorry," she whispered, "I'm sorry—"

Natalie produced a box of tissues. "Here. Blow."

Linda Harper sat straight and made an effort to control herself. "I'm all right now, honest. Thanks."

"My next class isn't until one," Natalie said, "so you and I will go to my apartment, where you will go to bed and get some sleep. I'll also call a friend of mine who's a doctor to come and make professional noises at you. Here—put your coat on and let's go while we can sneak out with no questions asked."

"Why are you bothering with me, Mrs. Keith?"

The question, as abrupt as it was honest, startled her. "I don't know," she answered more truthfully than she liked to admit. "If I ever figure it out, I'll let you know."

It was almost one o'clock when Natalie, having left Linda Harper asleep in her apartment, got back to her office. She

111

found a message that Chris Jensen had called, and hastily phoned him back.

"Well," he asked, "did someone lock the broom closet?"

"I had to go home. Any news on your end?"

"I'm not sure. Look—can you come over here after your next class?"

"I don't know why not. You sound worried, Chris."

"I had such a nice little jigsaw puzzle," he answered obliquely, "and it's beginning to fall apart. Do come, Natalie, and help me put it back together."

"I'll be there by two-thirty." She hung up, wondering what he meant.

She began to understand when she walked into his office and saw Will Gregg's little gold hammer on Jensen's desk.

"You found it! Where?"

"A person named Steinhoffer walked up and handed it to Detective Slocum, who gave it to me at precisely ten-twenty-six this morning."

"Steinhoffer?" Natalie repeated. "Wolfgang Steinhoffer? But he's one of Will's neighbors."

"Yeah." Jensen ground out his cigarette. "He's also a carpenter by trade. Doctor Gregg gave him the hammer two weeks ago to have a new handle made. It wasn't even in the house when he was murdered."

Natalie stiffened as the word cut her feelings like a lash. Will Gregg had been murdered, and they still didn't know why or by whom. Now they didn't even know how.

"Well," she said, "this does complicate things."

"It do, indeed it do. Look, Natalie, how much time have you?"

"How much do you need?"

He looked nervously at his watch. "I'm expecting what may be a pair of witnesses, the couple who live across the street from Doctor Gregg. It was they who called the precinct about his door's being open, and, according to Turk, they also saw someone leave the house at about the time Peter Archer claims he left. It's not exactly kosher, but I'd like you to hear what they have to say."

Natalie nodded, and they talked of other things until Turk Harrison arrived with the witnesses. She recognized them as James and Etta Fuller, people with whom Will had been no more than remotely friendly, and who had a reputation for neighborly espionage.

"You, ah, involved in this business, Professor?" James Fuller asked, staring at her.

"Doctor Keith," Jensen said firmly, "represents the University. Now then, sir, can you tell me what time it was when you saw this person leave Doctor Gregg's house? And was it a man or a woman?"

"You don't waste time, do you?" Fuller asked. "Come right to the point. Well, so'll I. It was nine-fifteen. Commercial had just come on TV, and I got up to rest my eyes. It was a man, by the way."

"We were watching that new Western," his wife added. "You know—'Guns of the Law.' It's not very good."

"Not many are, these days." Jensen smiled. "What else can you tell me about what you saw, Mr. Fuller?"

"Well," Fuller began, "I'd got up to stretch and was walking by our front window when I saw Gregg's porch light go on. I wouldn't have noticed it, mind, except that I was walking by the front window—"

"Of course not." Jensen smiled again, with what Natalie had come to think of as his jailside manner. "What did you happen to notice next?"

"Way-ul"—Fuller wet his lips—"I saw the door open and two men standing there. One of 'em was Gregg—he was in shirt sleeves—and the other had on a short jacket. Like one of them Eisenhower jackets. They talked a while, then the fella in the jacket left."

"Could you identify this 'man in the jacket' if you saw him again?"

Fuller shrugged. "Don't know. Nothing unusual about him. Just a fella in a jacket. Come to think of it, he had a case of some sort. One of them square, hard ones like the big shots carry their lunches in."

"An attaché case?" Jensen prompted.

113

"I guess that's what you call 'em. It was light-colored, I remember that."

"But there was nothing else—"

"Nope."

Natalie, struck by a sudden, desperate thought, scribbled a note and handed it to Jensen. He read it slowly, folded it, and stuck it into his pocket.

"Was the man with the case tall or short, Mr. Fuller?" he asked. "In general, how would you say he was built?"

Fuller was silent, picking his front teeth with his thumbnail. "Tall," he answered, "about like you, only a little heavier. Darker, too, I'd say. Looked like any of them college boys."

"I see." Jensen nodded solemnly. "Did he and Doctor Gregg shake hands?"

Fuller stopped picking his teeth and stared thoughtfully at Jensen. "Yeah. Yeah, they did. Funny thing, too. The young fella shook lefty. Shifted his case to his right hand and shook lefty."

"Like this?" Jensen asked, turning his hand thumb down. "Eh-huh."

"Then what?" he pressed on. "Which way did the young man go when he left?"

"Dunno," Fuller said. "Damned commercial was over and I went back to watch TV."

"You didn't notice if he had a car, of if he walked away—"

"Nope."

"I see. Well, thank you Mr. Fuller. You've been a great help to us. Now, if you and Mrs. Fuller will go with Sergeant Harrison, he'll explain about your statements. It won't take long, I promise."

"That's all?" Fuller asked.

"For now." Jensen repeated his brilliant smile. "You've helped us a lot, and we're grateful. Lucky for us you don't like TV commercials!"

To Natalie's astonishment, Fuller blushed. "Glad to help," he said. "It's been nice meeting you, Captain. Nice to see you too, Professor."

Natalie smiled. "We must get together sometime, under less dramatic circumstances."

Fuller agreed and followed his wife and Turk Harrison out of the room. Jensen licked his forefinger and marked an invisible X in the air.

"Score one for Keith," he said. "It looks as if Doctor Gregg was alive when Archer left by the front door."

Natalie did not smile. "There's a catch in that, even if I can't put my finger on it. May I see Peter?"

Jensen picked up his phone and asked to have Archer brought to his office. Listening to him, Natalie realized that she was tense to the point of rigidity and made a conscious effort to relax.

"Chris," she said, "are you thinking what I'm thinking?"

"That perhaps the incredible is true?"

"He could have had important information," she reasoned, "not necessarily even secret stuff—just something that would fill in a hole in somebody's report."

Jensen spoke somberly. "I hate to admit it, Nat, but I'm beginning to think it's possible and that I'm in over my head. Way over my head."

"What'll you do?"

He shrugged. "Become an actor, put on a good show for the newspapers while the FBI or some other set of initials does the real job. I trust you too are a disciple of Thespis—"

"I've had my moments," she answered. "Chris, I'm scared—"

"I know, but we've got to stand on our little flat feet and wait to see what the Feds produce. In the meantime"—he shrugged—"on with our own little researches."

"Meaning?"

"I wish I knew. Captain Hayes is starting to growl and the Press is about to start riding me with spurs. I just hope no one else gets burgled or murdered before we get a break, or we'll have a Jack the Ripper scare for sure."

Of a sudden, she admired him and his kind enough to forgive them their cynicism, their hardness, even their occasional falls from honor. Theirs was a tough, sordid, and dangerous profession, and it seemed to show only the least admirable side of anyone it dealt with. Because Chris Jensen couldn't catch a murderer in seven days he would receive the left-handed blessing of every newspaper in the county. Yet if this same Chris Jensen should someday take a bullet in the head, the same newspapers would note the fact in passing and forget it the next day. He was, after all, just a policeman—just a cop: a man who was a nuisance when he did his job and a menace when he could not.

The office door opened and a guard brought in Peter Archer. Natalie looked up, not knowing what to expect, and was relieved to see him neatly dressed and clean-shaven, albeit drawn and with dark smudges of fatigue under his eyes. The right sleeve of his jacket, hanging limp, made him seem defenseless and vulnerable.

"Professor Keith," he said, stopping short and blinking at her, "what're you doing here?"

"Checking up on you," She tried to sound casual. "Are you all right—anything you need?"

"Yeah"—he smiled—"a hacksaw!"

"Settle for a file?" She was aware that her voice lacked lightness.

"Why not? I've been kicked out of school, haven't I?"

"If you have, it's news to me."

He took the cigarette Jensen offered and nodded his thanks. "I didn't kill him, Mrs. Keith," he said, "please believe me. He and you are about the only friends I've got."

"Pete"—she looked straight at him—"if I thought for one moment that you'd killed Will Gregg, I wouldn't be here."

"No," he answered soberly, "I don't suppose you would. I'm awfully sorry it had to happen to him."

"So'm I, Pete, so am I. Lieutenant, may I ask him what happened between him and Will?"

"Please," Jensen said.

"I've told it so often I'm beginning to dream about it," Archer sighed. "The trouble is, nothing happened, and that's the God's truth, Professor. I've had trouble this semester—which you know as well as anybody—and Doctor Gregg was trying to help me figure out why. So help me, that's all we talked about."

116

"I heard you had an argument."

"I hadn't studied for an exam—yours, as a matter of fact—and he got on me about it. I guess I blew, but I deserved everything he said. When I went to his place that night we didn't talk about that at all."

Natalie relaxed and sat back in her chair. It was like Will to upbraid the boy for bad work one day and help him out the next. "Where did you go after you left Will—Doctor Gregg?"

"I decided to drive out to the Wilds," Archer said. "I wanted to think, and that's a good place for it."

The Wilds, Natalie knew, was one of the many unofficial names given to Mountainside State Park, a forty-square-mile stretch of virgin forest to the south of the city. Only one road led through it, and the state did everything possible to keep it as it had been when the first settlers arrived.

"How long were you there, Pete?"

"I never got there." He put out his cigarette. "I had a flat just this side of the entrance, and hadn't a flashlight so I just thrashed around in the dark trying to change it. I broke my hook when the damned—excuse me—when the wheel slipped and got away from me."

"No one came to help?"

"Not at that hour of the night, in October."

"Where'd you leave your tire to be fixed?" Jensen asked suddenly.

"I didn't," Archer answered. "Like I said, it got away from me and rolled down a hill. It's still out there, somewhere. The other cop—what's his name, Harriman?—said he'd try to find it, but I don't know if he did nor not."

"See what I mean?" Jensen turned to Natalie as if to appeal to her. "It's just fuzzy enought to be true."

"Hey," Archer asked, "whose side are you on, anyhow?"

"Yours," Jensen answered, "if it really happened the way you say."

"I'll take his word for it, Chris," Natalie said, "I know Pete, and I knew Will. Everything Pete's told us fits. Did Turk find the tire?"

Jensen shook his head. "We're short of men. Turk went out alone, but found nothing."

Natalie scowled and pressed her lips tightly together. "Pete, have you any idea where you lost the wheel? Did you see anything we could use as a landmark?"

Archer shook his head wearily. "I wish I had, but after I broke the hook, I got so mad I'm afraid I forgot everything. It's not easy to change a tire in the dark with one hand."

"It's hard enough with two in broad daylight," she agreed, "but you know how important this is—"

He looked at her, and for the first time she saw fear in his eyes. "I don't want to hang, Professor," he said softly. "I don't care how I've loused up my life, I don't want to hang."

"You won't." Jensen's tone caused Natalie to look up sharply. "We use the electric chair."

"Thanks," Archer said bitterly, "what do you do as an encore—bite someone?"

"No, I send you back to your cell. You're finished with him, aren't you, Natalie?"

She nodded silently, her mind working quickly to try to understand Jensen's slip—if slip it had been. To her, James Fuller's testimony had cleared Peter Archer of all suspicion, and she wondered if Jensen were beginning to plot his "act" for the newspapers. If he were, it meant that he was beginning to believe in Will Gregg's involvement with spies and counter-spies. As for herself, much as she longed to accept this *deus ex machina,* she could not.

It just doesn't wash, she thought; I don't know why, but it doesn't. It's like the old joke about the coin marked '12 B.C.'— it can't be that easy.

The missing wheel was the key to it, she decided. If that could be found it would prove that Peter had been far from Will Gregg's house at the time of the murder. Or would it? There would still be no proof that the wheel had been lost when Peter claimed—or how he claimed.

"What grim thought are you cherishing?" Jensen asked after Archer was out of earshot.

"I was thinking about coins," she answered, "specifically,

118

about a hoard I found once in Palestine. They came from four different kingdoms and spanned almost a century of time. As a matter of fact, it took me almost six months to identify and date them all."

"So?"

"The point is, I could set a period before which the hoard couldn't have been buried, but *not* the date after which— Do you follow me?"

"Frankly—no."

"Empty your pockets—well, the young man is wealthy!—now write down the date of each coin."

Reluctantly at first, but then with interest, Jensen obeyed. After several minutes he shoved a sheet of paper across his desk to her.

"There," he said, "one half dollar and two quarters too worn to date; one 1934 penny; one dime, two pennies, and a nickel dated 1953; two quarters, a dime, and three pennies from 1958; one white penny left over from World War II and dated 1943; and a 1956 dime. What's that supposed to prove?"

"What year is this?"

"Nineteen-sixty— Oh." He cocked his head and dragged down the corners of his mouth. "I see what you're driving at. If you found those coins buried somewhere, you'd have to conclude that they were buried no earlier than nineteen-fifty-eight—two years ago."

"Christopher, you may go to the head of the class. And if the time gap can be that big in the twentieth century, with the great volume of coins struck each year, think what it could be in the first century B.C."

"Did it matter that you couldn't date your hoard?"

She shrugged. "It might've, it just might've. There was archaeological evidence on the site of burning, and some vague literary evidences of an abortive revolt against Roman authority. If we could've connected this with the hoard, and the hoard with the burning—well, it wouldn't have rewritten history, but it would've made an interesting footnote."

"But all you could fix was the downward date," he repeated,

his interest kindling, "the date before which it couldn't have been buried."

"That much, so help me, I had. Do you realize that you have *both* brackets for Peter's whereabouts last Wednesday night?"

Once again she saw him turn his thoughts inward, creating an insulating void between himself and the world. She shivered slightly, and sat as unmoving as she could.

"But the top one's weak, Natalie." The words came as an audible excerpt from his thoughts. "Fuller's statement fixes the downward limit, but there's a forty-five-minute span between the time Archer's roommate left and the time he got back to find Archer in the room. You can do a lot in three quarters of an hour."

"Can you drive from Will's house to the Wilds? Or back?"

"I don't know." He stood up. "Let's go find out."

"Now look," she warned, rising with him, "don't forget the difference in traffic conditions—"

He stopped short. "Who's the detective here, anyhow?"

"Well, you do outrank me—"

He grinned at her. "Nice of you to admit it! Let's go driving in the country."

It took them forty-four minutes to drive from Will Gregg's house through moderate traffic to the fringes of the Wilds. By Jensen's reckoning, this could be cut by a good twenty minutes at nine P.M., so that Archer, who had been seen leaving Gregg's house nine-fifteen, could have reached the same spot between nine-thirty-five and nine-forty-five, and still have had time to fix his tire and get to South Hall some time between ten and ten-forty-five.

"That's tighter than I thought it'd be," Natalie said with satisfaction, checking her calculations against Jensen's.

"If he was really here."

She stared at him. "I'm trying to decide if that remark comes under the heading of skepticism or cynicism."

"I'm a cop," he answered, avoiding her eyes and looking off into the forest. "If we can find proof that he was here, splendid.

120

If not, as far as I'm concerned, he wasn't here. This road isn't heavily traveled at this time of year, and it hasn't rained for a week, so the shoulder may still show where he stopped."

"I know," Natalie inserted, "'*if* he stopped.' We know his wheel got away from him and rolled downhill, so we can eliminate the flat stretches—"

"Great," Jensen said dryly, "have you driven this road lately? It follows the shoulders of the hills for about seventy-five per cent of its length."

Natalie was thoughtful. "Look, Chris, you managed to produce an airplane without difficulty. How about a helicopter?"

"Now don't tell me you fly one of those too!"

"Not legally, yet." She winked at him. "But pictures taken from a chopper might show where Pete stopped. They might even show the track left by the rolling wheel. That grass looks dead enough to hold an impression for a week."

"I'm beginning to think," Jensen growled, "that you're in the wrong profession!"

"There's a little detective in all archaeologists, plus a little burglar."

"Perhaps," he suggested, "you should write a book entitled *Tombs I Have Burgled*. The trouble is, Nat, I'll have trouble getting the captain to take me seriously."

"Even if I produce those reconnaisance pictures of Italy that Major Muller mentioned yesterday?"

"Even if Cecil B. DeMille produced them."

"Try, Chris," she pleaded, "please try."

He started the car, made a smooth U turn, and started back toward the city. "You realize, of course, that having as good as eliminated Archer as a suspect, we're now stuck with Enemy Agent X. It doesn't make sense, Natalie."

"Does the human race ever make sense, Christopher?"

"I'm beginning to wonder."

They lapsed into brief silence, and when they spoke again it was, by mutual if tacit consent, of sports and the weather. Natalie found herself assessing the quality of the University's basketball team, which she had never seen in action, and Jensen soberly agreed that its chances were not the best. Only when he stopped before her apartment did he bring back the subject of police work.

"Look, Natalie," he said tentatively, "could you be at Doctor Gregg's house at eight-thirty tonight? We're going to try something—and there are still loose ends to be knotted."

She felt herself stiffen, and it was a moment before she trusted herself to speak. "I don't know why not, Chris."

"I'd feel better if you were there, if only because you know all the personalities involved"—he smiled lopsidedly—"including me."

Yes, she thought; including you. The trouble is, I'm also fond of everyone—including you. And I loved Will, with all my heart I loved him. Lord, how tangled can emotions get?

"I'll be there," she promised, "unless I get hit by a truck."

"Heaven forbid! Call me there if you can't make it."

"Sure." She got out and closed the car door. "See you later."

He gave her a casual salute and started away. She stood for a moment, looking after him and thinking of nothing in particular, and then went inside. There was still, she reminded herself, the problem of Linda Harper, the confused and unhappy girl upstairs in her apartment. She walked quickly to the switchboard, where she had left her keys for the doctor, and then went upstairs.

The apartment was silent and remained so even after she turned on the living-room light. In the middle of the coffee table a note was propped against an ashtray, and she opened it quickly.

I've looked over your stray pup, [she read], and can find nothing particularly wrong. Gave her something which should keep her asleep until morning, but may not. What she needs more than anything is what you've given her—a little warmth and personal interest. Some parents don't deserve children, do they?

So—when are us Hollanders going to see you? Nonprofessionally, that is. Mike agrees with me that you should do something about that back before it really gives you trouble. I don't know where you got the idea that a woman of your age could dig ditches like a construction worker!

Give us a call—preferably home

Peg

"Woman of [my] age" indeed! Natalie thought irritably; who does Peg Hollander think *she* is, Peter Pan?

Still grumbling, Natalie went into the kitchen to get something for supper. Peg Hollander might not be a psychiatrist, but she was a good doctor, and her findings on Linda Harper were reassuring.

She opened a can of spaghetti, poured it carefully into a pan, and then knocked the empy can to the floor with her elbow. It was possible, she concluded, staring morosely at the spots on her kitchen floor, that Linda Harper wasn't the only member of the household whose emotions were flapping like storm signals. The trouble was, she decided, kneeling to wipe up, that her feelings were more in hiding than rampant. The smash might come later.

Yet somehow she doubted it. The thing that impressed and confused her most was that while she could accept the idea of working with the police to catch Will's murderer, she could not accept the fact of Will's murder. Between the acknowledgment of truth and the acceptance of its meaning there seemed to be a great gulf fixed that admitted to no bridging.

CHAPTER X

She had just finished supper when the phone rang loudly. She caught it on the third ring and asked, breathless and subdued, who was calling.

"Edward Ken," the caller answered. "What've you been doing—push-ups?"

"Darn near it," she panted. "I've a friend staying with me for a few days who isn't well, and I was afraid the phone would wake her. Is there something I can do for you?"

"There certainly is. Michi and I were wondering if you could come over this evening. I just got a rather interesting new recording of the Beethoven Ninth."

Natalie groaned. "I'd like nothing better, but I have to— I've an appointment with Lieutenant Jensen."

"Again?"

"Still."

He was silent briefly, and Natalie could almost feel his disapproval. For an instant, fleeting and unique, she shared it.

"Are they still holding young Archer?" he asked.

"Yes, but—" She hesitated. "I can't explain it, but he hasn't been charged with the murder."

"Oh. You mean they're holding him as a material witness?"

"I haven't the faintest idea, Edward. I seem incapable of understanding any law more modern than Hammurabi."

Edward Ken laughed, and Natalie shivered. He sounded so like Will Gregg when he laughed.

"That's the trouble with you archaeologists," he said, "you're *dedicated*. Now an anthropologist would hide behind some statement about not having had time to do a comparative study on the laws of selected cultures pertaining to murder and/or mayhem. You're sure you can't make it tonight? Won't the law be finished with you by nine?"

"I'm afraid not."

"Ah, well," he sighed, "better luck next time. Michi says hello."

"Hello right back. I'll see you tomorrow, and thanks for thinking of me. It sounds like a good recording."

She put the phone down, turned to go back to the kitchen, and jumped in surprise to see Linda Harper standing at the end of the short hallway. "Good heavens, you startled me! Are you all right?"

"Yes, ma'am. I didn't mean to eavesdrop, honest, I was just looking for the—"

"It's thataway." Natalie smiled. "Come to the kitchen afterward and have a cup of tea with me."

She looks better, Natalie thought as Linda, pink with embarrassment, went her way; maybe all she needed was a few hours' sleep. Funny how the reactions of youth, like those of old age, run to extremes. The young still enjoy the sublime self-assurance of inexperience, and the ancient just lose their inhibitions. It's those of us in the middle who seem most bound by the convention of self-control. "Moderation in all things" is pure eyewash. Where in all literature do you find greater emotional excess than in Greek tragedy? Of course it's used creatively, to discipline the mind and cleanse the soul, while nowadays we wallow in it like pigs in a mud puddle. . . .

A timid knock interrupted her thoughts, and she looked up to see Linda Harper. "Come in and sit down. How do you feel?"

"Much better, thanks, Mrs. Keith. Just"—she yawned—"a little groggy. I think it's what the doctor gave me. I could sleep for days and days—"

Natalie laughed and got a cup and saucer from the cabinet. "Hours, anyhow. Do you take lemon or milk with your tea? Or would you prefer instant coffee?"

"Well, if it's all right, could I have a glass of milk?"

"I think it can be arranged. By the way, Peg—Doctor Hollander—said you're fine. She just seemed to feel you'd been overdoing it a little."

"Not really," Linda said, "it's just that everything's come due at once, and I was behind to start. I don't know—I just can't seem to get organized this year."

"Are you still active in the Thespians?" Natalie asked. "I know you did a lot with them last year."

Linda shook her head. "There hasn't been time. Besides, I'm too tired. I wish I could, though," she added wistfully.

Natalie looked thoughtfully at her for a moment. Since she had come this far, she might as well try to go the second mile. "You're really interested in the theater, aren't you?"

The girl nodded. "I don't know why, really. I don't particularly like acting, but I love the theater. I thought maybe I'd try writing or criticism. I might even teach," she added.

Natalie deliberately put the milk carton back in the refrigerator and closed the door before she spoke again. "I've had an idea, Linda, something that might help with the work problem. You're going on to take the second semester of Ancient Civilizations, aren't you?"

"Yes."

"Good." Natalie smiled. "I hate to lose bright students. My idea is this—we'll forget the three term papers this semester if you'll undertake one long one on an assigned topic. If you can get it in before finals, fine—otherwise, I'll give you an incomplete and you can take a year."

Linda's eyes widened and she stared in bewilderment. "Are you kidding?" she blurted.

"No, I'm serious. The book of rules allows a teacher to give such leeway to students when there are—quote, extenuating circumstances, unquote—and I'd say you're about as extenuated as one person can get."

"I could have a whole *year?*"

"So say the powers that be," Natalie answered lightly, "only I reserve the right to assign the topic. I'd like to see you do something on the history of the theater, starting with Neanderthal man, if you dare, and working through to the fall of Rome."

Linda Harper's face, slightly flushed to begin, became suddenly radiant with excitement.

"You might start," Natalie said quickly to forestall an emotional outpouring, "by reading Henri Frankfort on the

Memphite theology and mystery plays. Then tackle Professor Marguerite Bieber's monumental work on the Greek theater. You might also pay passing respects to Sir Arthur Evans, J. D. S. Pendlebury, and E. K. Chambers, among others. But I warn you," she added sternly, "these are tough going."

"You don't care how I handle it?"

"As long as it's reasonably well written and you can back up your opinions and conclusions—no."

The girl began to talk, spreading ideas and questions before Natalie as before an oracle. It was as if a dazed mind had suddenly cleared and could begin to function again.

She's read a tremendous amount already, Natalie thought, listening; all it needs is organizing. God, how I wish Hugh Laurence could work on this one! I can make her a competent researcher and reporter, but he could make her a scholar. I wonder if there isn't some way . . .

"What do you think, Professor?" Linda asked.

Natalie, who had no idea of the question, smiled and shook her head. "I think you'd better go back to bed, and if you wake up during the night and find me not here, don't worry. I've an appointment that may keep me out late. See you in the morning."

Her appointment with Jensen was for eight-thirty, but Natalie arrived at Will Gregg's house at exactly eight twenty-four. She stood for a time on the sidewalk, hesitant to trespass on her own memories. Was it only a week? Only seven days? Or did she stand now, as she had so often in the past, on the threshold of a house that had known neither life nor love for tens of centuries?

In Pompeii, as here, the houses stood empty; their sherds and scraps of human life immured in ash within them. She had seen the plaster casts of long-vanished Pompeians, like ghosts solidified, making more real that brief moment of time that earth had preserved to itself. Now, standing before this house that she had once known so well, she thought it farther removed in time and meaning than the ruins of Pompeii.

When she finally went in, she found Chris Jensen already

there and busy on the telephone, and went into the living room after waving him a greeting. It was precisely as it had been a week ago: their three coffee containers still graced the wastepaper basket, and a fine coating of dust had settled on the tops of the tables and the arms of the chairs. Will's Morris chair, springs sagging and cushion unfluffed, waited by the fireplace as it always had.

Natalie walked toward it slowly, forcing herself to accept the pain of its emptiness. She ran a hesitant forefinger along the piping of the worn upholstery while the ghosts of her own past stirred under the fine and clinging dust of memory. Not all Pompeiis are ancient, or precise upon a map.

"I'm sorry, Nat," Jensen said quietly, "I didn't think it would hurt this much."

She smiled sadly without looking up. "It had to happen someday, Chris. Better sooner than later, probably."

"Yeah," he agreed dryly, "probably."

She turned abruptly and faced him, her whole manner changing as she moved. "What now, Mr. Holmes?" she asked brightly.

"An experiment," he answered. "Turk is across the street in the Fullers' living room, and two of my men are going to reenact what Archer and Doctor Gregg did last Thursday."

"You're half an hour early, or is that because of increased darkness?"

"Yes." He nodded. "Now—after the man playing Archer says good-by and leaves, he's going to try something."

"What?"

"If it works, you'll find out. At the same time the other man will take a car and head for the Wilds, drive in about as far as we did today, and then go back to South Hall."

"Meanwhile," Natalie asked, "we are doing—what?"

He hedged. "That depends. We'd better start."

She followed him out into the hall and stood watching two policemen go through the motions of saying good-by in the doorway. A few seconds later the front door closed again, and she heard a car start up and pull away. Other than that, nothing seemed to happen, though Jensen stood tense and expectant as if listening for something. After a time his look of expectancy hardened to one of concern and worry. Natalie watched in silence, wanting to ask questions but aware that she should not. Instead, she concentrated on receiving to herself as many impressions of the moment as possible without bothering to sort them.

A dog barked suddenly and was joined by another. Natalie recognized them, and located each on a mental map. "There's someone out back," she said, and heard a man's voice challenge the prowler.

Jensen turned, and she saw on his face a chain of subtle, unguarded expressions. Her own senses, already honed to a fine edge, quickened yet farther.

"That's Detective Sylvio. I was wondering if the dogs would notice him."

"Banjo barks even at me," Natalie told him, "and I've known him since he was a pup."

"How long before he gets bored?"

"Bored? Banjo? Not that dog, Chris."

"Who's the other hound?"

"A toy poodle in the house directly behind this one. She *will* get bored."

Jensen nodded and bit absently at his thumb knuckle as if trying to pull a splinter. "I think I'll leave Sylvio out there a while anyhow," he said, more to himself than to her, "on the off chance—"

Natalie knew suddenly what he had meant that morning when he had agreed that Will Gregg had been alive when Peter Archer left "by the front door." Between this house and its neighbor, the one harboring the suspicious Banjo, ran a gravel driveway that led to a little-used garage. The fence on Will's side was low and hedgeless.

The idea that Peter Archer might have circled back after leaving Will, slipped up the driveway and stepped over the fence into the back yard, was so appallingly obvious that Natalie felt stupid for not having thought of it sooner. But Jensen had thought of it—thought enough of it to send a detective prowling around in the dark to see if it were possible. The only snag was a tenaciously inquisitive mongrel dog named Banjo. Natalie blessed him with every bark.

Turk Harrison arrived unheralded and looking, Natalie thought, something less than cheerful. "Fuller has a photographic memory," he announced. "Except that we're half an hour early, his timetable is perfect."

"Score round two for Keith?" Natalie asked, and immediately wished she had not.

"Looks that way," Jensen agreed, "but round three depends on the man in the car. Any word from him yet, Turk?"

Harrison shook his head. "I thought I'd wait in the car until he calls, if it's okay with you."

Jensen nodded, chewing his thumb again. "I've a problem I need your help with, Natalie. Something of Doctor Gregg's that can't be found. I know it exists, but apparently it's lost somewhere."

She smiled. "Knowing Will's filing system, it could be anywhere. What is it?"

"A paper, probably typed but possibly partly handwritten. It's the codicil to his will. We learned of it yesterday when his attorney came back from vacation. He told us that he and Doctor Gregg had a long telephone conference three weeks ago, outlining changes he wanted made in the will. He also promised to send the lawyer a draft, but we can't find it. All we have are the lawyer's own notes."

Natalie looked wistful. "That's like Will, sending a draft of a legal document to a lawyer! Maybe he changed his mind and let the matter drop."

Jensen looked owlish. "Was he apt to do things like that?"

"There you go again with that boomerang in your voice. No—it isn't like him, but I suppose it could have happened."

"I don't think it did," Jensen said. "We found some shorthand notes in a stenographer's notebook that seem to deal with changes in a will, but unfortunately the next page is missing."

"Well then, Renata may have it. She sometimes takes—took—personal work of Will's home to do."

Jensen made his face blank and studied the tips of his fingers.

130

"We have a problem there, Natalie. Me and my humanitarian impulses! La Duval has made herself exceedingly scarce."

Natalie was thoughtfully silent, the tip of her tongue barely visible between her lips. "It's possible," she said judiciously, "that Will stuck the papers in a book somewhere, though precisely where I've no idea."

Jensen considered for a moment and then, as an afterthought, sent a man to ask Harrison if Duval had answered his telegrams. Then he went upstairs, followed by Natalie, whose time sense was oddly scrambled.

There's a pattern here, somewhere, she thought; if we could find it, we'd know the guilty from the innocent. There has to be a pattern—even in madness there's pattern—

Jensen opened the library door and snapped on the light. "Any suggestions?"

Natalie shook her head, thinking that he sounded like a small boy on his first scavenger hunt.

"He kept most of his personal papers in that locked file," Natalie recalled, "the one that was broken into."

"Do me a favor," Jensen said, sitting on the edge of the long table, "check the file for me."

Puzzled, she looked at him, then, with a slight shrug, went to the file and began to search. It took several minutes, but finally, more annoyed than anything else, she finished.

"Now tell me where else he kept things," Jensen said.

"You knew it wasn't there!"

"No, but I was pretty sure it wasn't."

"That was a dirty trick, Chris."

"It's a dirty business."

She looked at him as she would at a possibly forged antiquity, and suddenly a series of questions that could have been traps sparked in her memory. Why had there been a policeman outside her apartment building for three days last week? Why had he gone to such lengths to cultivate her friendship?

"Do something for me, Chris?"

"If I can—"

"You can, if you will." Everything inside her went taut in her efforts at self-control. "Before I conclude I've gone com-

131

pletely paranoid, tell me honestly if I'm a suspect in this 'dirty business.'"

"The possibility did cross my mind," he answered frankly, "but that wasn't why I had you check the file. After all, you're the only one of us who knew Doctor Gregg. Presumably you also know something about his filing system."

"You're hedging," she accused.

Jensen smiled and pulled the wrapper off a pack of cigarettes. "No, Professor"—he offered her one—"you are not now—nor ever have been, seriously—a suspect. You had neither opportunity nor, as far as we could find, motivation."

She accepted his answer as reasonable, and tried to think. "I didn't find his 'Personal' file," she said, "Renata may have taken it home with her and forgotten to tell you. After all, with her brother-in-law, or whatever, getting sick . . ."

"Sounds possible." He got up from his perch. "We don't need to wait around here; let's go to the Duval household and see what we can find. I'd like you to come, Natalie, but it's not mandatory."

"My," she mocked, "such big words! I've decided I like traveling with policemen. It gives one a remarkable sense of security."

Jensen laughed soundlessly. "Then let's go. You're sure there's no other place here that the papers might be?"

"The middle desk drawer, maybe, but if you don't mind, I'd rather not—that mixture of pencil stubs, rocks, and odd papers was so much Will."

"I've gone through the desk drawers myself, Nat," he said gently. "I meant in the attic, or a closet or something."

"Oh. Well, you might find a meteorite in the closet or a stuffed raccoon in the attic, but not papers. Will had his own scholarly and slightly idiotic way of organizing things."

Jensen moved toward the door. "We'll find Turk," he said, "and go see what the Duval establishment has to offer. I hope the niece doesn't make me go chasing after a search warrant."

Natalie stopped and looked at him with a peculiar expression of surprise and shock. "Could she?"

"Oh yes. People get defensive about policemen, even when they have nothing to hide."

"I can understand that with people born in Europe," she said thoughtfully, "but not with native Americans. Shades of Himmler and Beria—"

Turk Harrison, looking annoyed and worried, was starting up the stairs as they started down. He stopped and waited for them.

"What's gnawing on you?" Jensen asked.

"That telegram," he said, "no answer. I checked with the company, and they said they weren't able to deliver it, so I checked with the telephone company—"

"And there's no such address, right?"

Harrison pushed his fingers through his thick, dark hair and nodded gloomily.

Jensen, still standing two steps above his partner, was silent and grim. "Well," he said finally, "at least I've no one to blame but myself. I was the one who decided to let her go. Turk, call the office and ask Charlie to contact the New Orleans police. It's their problem now."

"May I say something, Chris?" Natalie asked. "Renata's done work for me from time to time, and I've noticed that she has a tendency to scramble numbers. Maybe she gave you the right address, but backward."

Jensen looked at Harrison, who shook his head. "I thought of that, so I had the long-distance operator check every Endicot in the book. No luck."

"One thing about it"—Jensen walked down the last two steps —"when a Jensen goofs, it's spectacular. Let's hope we can find something at the Duval establishment."

It was a five-minute drive to Renata Duval's apartment in what had once been a fashionable 'park-garden' development. Now, however, its glamour had tarnished and mellowed to solid respectability. Retired people and businesswomen of all ages enjoyed its Georgian architecture and grassy quadrangles. As they approached up a long brick walk Natalie wondered how the staid and presumably conservative inhabitants regarded Renata Duval and her philosophical oddities.

"Do you know which building she's in?" Jensen asked.

"No," she answered, "I've never been here before. In fact, I'm thoroughly lost."

Jensen grinned. "Your apartment house is that way, a good brisk twenty-minute walk."

Natalie closed her eyes and shook her head. "Remind me to brush up on celestial navigation! I'd hate to get this scrambled in the air."

"I'll say one thing for Duval," Turk Harrison commented, "she's not underpaid."

"It is a pretty classy slum," Jensen agreed.

"Actually," Natalie told them, "she shares her apartment with her niece, who also works. And she types theses and manuscripts for such of us as are nuts enough to write 'em."

They found the building and the apartment without difficulty, and Jensen's ring was answered by a slender young woman whose ivory and ebony coloring left both men momentarily speechless.

"You must be Carla," Natalie said, charging into the breach. "I'm Natalie Keith, an acquaintance of your aunt's—"

Carla Duval smiled charmingly and opened the door. "Aunt Rene's spoken of you many times, Professor. Do come in—and your gentlemen friends."

Natalie smiled benignly at the fidgeting detectives. "Miss Duval," she said properly, "may I present Lieutenant Jensen and Sergeant Harrison, both of the police."

"I had hoped this was a social call." Carla Duval offered her hand. "It's been lonely since Aunt Rene went South. Is there something you gentlemen wanted to know?"

"In a way, Miss Duval," Jensen answered, following her into the living room. "Actually, it's about some work your aunt may have been doing for Doctor Gregg at the time of his death."

The girl's eyes widened and she stared at him. "I wouldn't know anything about that. Aunt Rene and I never talk business."

"Do you also work for the University, Miss Duval?"

"No, I'm a teller in a bank."

Jensen started to ask her something else, but stopped at the sight of a man standing in the living room. Carla Duval smiled

134

charmingly again and introduced him as Ramón Santiago, law student and Cuban refugee.

"Ramón's father and mine were friends," she explained, "so when he fled Cuba and came here, Aunt Rene agreed to help him find work."

"I'm glad you're here," Natalie said as the young man bowed over her hand, "I visited your lovely country once, in less unhappy times."

"We are used to sadness, Señora," he said, "but you are right. This is the saddest of times. But someday it will be better."

"Now then"—Carla Duval resumed the role of hostess—"I know that these gentlemen can't enjoy spirits with us, but perhaps coffee?"

"Thank you"—Jensen managed to sound shy and authoritative at the same time—"but we haven't time. As Mrs. Keith explained, we're trying to find some papers of Doctor Gregg's that we know your aunt was typing—or had typed—at the time of his death. They're in a filing folder marked 'Personal.' I wonder if you'd mind checking your aunt's desk to see if it's there."

"Of course," Carla said, "I won't be a minute—"

She left, and the three men made a fumbling attempt at conversation. For some reason their exchange of courtesies began to irk Natalie beyond bearing, and she deliberately shunted her attention to the room itself and its furnishings. After a moment she ceased to be particularly aware of the halting, self-conscious conversation in the background.

Renata Duval's taste in decoration was outwardly modern, but hinted of something else that could have been Louis XIV or updated baroque. Whatever it was, Natalie sensed a wrongness, a lack of harmony and cohesion in the room. The color scheme, leaning to earth colors—browns, reds, and oranges—was satisfactory, but something was out of place, somewhere.

It was, she decided, the fireplace. Its lines were basically wrong, its proportion too differently scaled, to accept the style of furniture arranged around it. Nor did it help that the mantel was covered with reproductions of well-known sculpture. Perhaps that was the trouble. There was a head of a young boy

135

that might be a Donatello, a study of hands by Rodin, a bust of Albert Schweitzer, an Egyptian hawk—

Natalie's eye stopped and clung to the hawk. If that was a reproduction, it was certainly the best she had ever seen.

"I'm terribly sorry, Lieutenant," Carla Duval said loudly, "but there's no file on Aunt Rene's desk and none in her briefcase. Could it be in Doctor Gregg's office at the University?"

"We'll check again," Jensen answered, getting up, "and thank you for your trouble. By the way, you don't by any chance have your aunt's address, do you? We seem to have the wrong one."

Carla's eyes widened again, and Natalie, her attention divided between the mantel and the speakers, wondered vaguely if the girl were aware of the effect this expression had on others.

"It sounds silly, I guess," Carla admitted, "but I don't really know where she is. You see, I've never been to New Orleans. All I know is that she's staying with her brother-in-law and his baby while Aunt Marie is in the hospital."

"We have an address"—Jensen read if off—"but," he added, seeing her nod in agreement, "we aren't sure of the spelling of his name. We have Marvin Endicot, with one 't.' Is that right?"

The expressive eyes were momentarily wary. "Yes, only one 't.' Rather affected, isn't it?"

"I once knew a man who spelled Jones with a 'z,'" Jensen said. "Thanks very much for your time, Miss Duval. We'll be on our way."

His words registered on Natalie's awareness, and she got up with an automatic expression of thanks and started toward the front door. It really was an extraordinary reproduction.

"I'll lay a bet," Turk Harrison said as they walked across the well-lit quadrangle toward the street, "that there's no such person as Marvin Endicot, with one or two 't.'s.'"

"I'd rather know if that codicil still exists," Jensen answered. "I wonder what bank the girl works for. Doctor Gregg used the State Trust."

"It can't have vanished," Natalie reasoned, coming briefly out of her silence, "though it seems to have, doesn't it?"

Jensen made an indefinite sound in reply, and said nothing more. All three of them, reacting in their own ways to the interview, were similarly abstracted and still: the detectives ostensibly because of a missing document; Natalie for a reason that would have seemed absurd to them.

For her, the sticking point was the Egyptian hawk on Renata Duval's mantel. Even at half a room's distance, she had recognized it as unlike the other statuary. Now, in the open air where there was nothing to distract her, she knew she must see it again at close range.

"Oh damn," she said aloud, "I've left my gloves! You two go on about your business. I'll go back and get them."

"We'll wait."

"That's silly, Chris," she protested, "it's not ten yet, and there are plenty of cabs. If I'm idiot enough to leave things lying about, it serves me right to pay my way home. Call me in the morning and let me know how things turn out, will you?"

"Sure," he said, "and if you have any bright ideas, call me. Good night, Nat, and take care."

It occurred to Natalie as she rode up again in the elevator that she should have told Jensen her suspicions; that the police were, after all, the proper ones to conduct investigations. But it was too late now, and she would have to finish what she had begun.

Carla Duval was obviously surprised to see her, and Natalie apologized profusely for her return. "I had an afterthought, Miss Duval," she explained. "It occurred to me that your aunt might have finished typing Will's—Doctor Gregg's—papers, and been about to mail them when she was called away. I wonder if you'd mind checking her briefcase and the desk again for a large Manila envelope—possibly addressed to an attorney or to his bank."

"There was an envelope, I remember," Carla said. "Go on into the living room, Professor, and I'll check. It'll only take a minute."

Relieved and eager, Natalie forced herself to walk slowly down the long hall. The living room was empty, and she had a sudden irrational feeling that the *deus ex machina* had appeared and taken control of the situation. Without hesitation she went to the mantel and took down the Egyptian hawk. With surging excitement, she realized that the piece was not a reproduction, but an original.

"Looking for something, Professor?" a man's voice asked.

Her immediate reaction was to gasp in enough air to scream, but she forced herself to turn slowly and smile.

"Not exactly, Mr. Santiago," she said, "I was really looking *at* something. You see, it occurred to me that the papers Lieutenant Jensen wants may be in an envelope among Renata's things, so I came back and asked Carla to check. While I was waiting I got curious and decided to have a closer look at this." She held up the Egyptian hawk. "It's—most interesting, really."

Santiago sat down and produced an ivory holder into which he fitted a cigarette. "I am fond of Renata, but there is something about her and people like her which I do not understand." He belatedly offered Natalie a cigarette, which she refused. "What I mean is this," he continued, "this—how do you call it?— passion for collecting copies of works of art. In a way they are like children, clipping pretty pictures out of magazines."

"Personally," Natalie countered, "I'm glad to see signs of interest in art, even when it lacks coherence."

"I'm sorry, Professor," Carla said from the hall. "I can't find any envelope like you described in— Oh, Ramón. I thought you'd left."

Santiago smiled and lit his cigarette. "I forgot my gloves and came back for them."

Natalie went stiff inside and felt the pulse beating in her throat. It might be coincidence, she reminded herself, but was it? Was it likely that she and Ramón Santiago would seize on the same excuse for returning to this apartment after they had left it?

Carla Duval still hesitated in the doorway as if sensing that something was not right about this gathering.

"I hope you'll forgive my bad manners," Natalie said as lightly as she could, "but I couldn't resist a closer look at this Horus. I'm an archaeologist, you know."

"It's new." Carla still lingered in the doorway. "Aunt Rene brought it home the other day. I don't know where she got it. It's not like those other reproductions."

138

"Perhaps," Santiago suggested, "because it isn't a reproduction."

Natalie looked sharply at him, and he smiled.

"I too have seen the little red numbers, Professor, the same kind that one sees on pieces in a museum. Can you tell us what they mean?"

"They're registration numbers," she answered, fighting to stay calm. "If you know how to read them they'll tell you the year a piece was found, the exact location of the find, and the number of the logbook in which it's recorded."

"And where does that thing come from?"

"Nubia, Mr. Santiago. It was found in nineteen-forty-seven, by me."

"But surely you are mistaken—"

I wish I knew how to play chess, Natalie thought irrelevantly; I wish I knew what he's trying to do.

"I also," she went on aloud, "gave it to Doctor Gregg. It was in his study until last week. It seems to have disappeared between noon of the day he was killed and the time the police asked me to check his collection for missing items. Naturally," she added, "I was somewhat surprised to find it here."

Carla Duval's face went ashen and she sat down heavily in the nearest chair.

"It seems Miss Duval has read my mind," Natalie said.

Santiago repeated the ritual of filling his cigarette holder. "So have I, Professor, and you have—to put it delicately—created something of a problem for me. You see, it would be highly embarrassing for me should the police learn of this—ah—theory of yours."

"And what," Natalie asked, "makes you believe that they don't?"

Santiago lit his cigarette, returned the lighter to his pocket, and brought his hand out again with a small automatic pistol balanced casually in it.

"I don't think they do, Professor. You hardly had time to tell them."

"So you did follow us out."

"Down the service stairs, yes. I was standing about ten feet away when you announced the loss of your gloves."

Natalie smiled and bowed slightly toward him. "You're an excellent actor, Mr. Santiago, but do you realize that you've lost your Cuban accent in the past five minutes?"

Carla Duval twisted around in her chair and stared at him. "My God, Ramón—"

He flicked the gun toward her and she was still. "I do not understand you, Professor," he said, returning his attention to Natalie, "don't you realize that you're getting yourself deeper and deeper into trouble every time you open your mouth?"

"Yes," Natalie answered, "but then, I was in trouble the moment I walked in, wasn't I? Actually, Mr. Santiago, I'm following a variety of the scientific method. You puzzle me, and I'm trying to find out what you have to do with whatever's going on."

Santiago showed his teeth in a parody of a smile. "Let's call it a business venture, Professor. I'm a firm believer in private enterprise."

"Ah yes," Natalie said, surprised by her own calmness, "and I've started a panic in the stock market."

Santiago started to say something, but shrugged.

"And of course," she went on, "something will have to be done about me. Are you planning to shoot me here, or somewhere else?"

"A wise man," Santiago countered, "never shoots the friend of a cop, especially one who teaches early-morning classes."

Natalie tried to swallow, but found her mouth too dry. "You're very efficient, Mr. Santiago."

He smiled again, and she knew that he had sensed her growing fear. "Have you ever had an accident in that airplane of yours, Professor? Of course I don't know much about flying, but it seems I've read something about ice being a danger to small planes at this time of year."

"It happens occasionally," she acknowledged. "Where am I going—New Orleans?"

Santiago laughed. "I wish we had met under other conditions,

140

Professor! No, I think you will decide to take a brief leave of absence—to 'get away from it all,' as it were."

"Why not say I'm going home to Connecticut to spend some time with my brother?"

"Why not? You are too helpful, Professor. Now you, Carla, my dear, will stay here and say nothing. Remember that you're in this as deeply as I am—or as your dear, mad Aunt Renata. No one is likely to believe you innocent."

"Do I infer from that, Mr. Santiago," Natalie asked, "that you killed Doctor Gregg?"

He reacted sharply and with alarm. "I didn't. I couldn't have. I was in New York and I can prove it."

"But you did take his papers—"

He relaxed visibly. "No, Professor," he answered patiently, "I didn't take the papers. I found them. And being as I said a businessman, I decided to take advantage of the opportunity."

"Even if it was illegal."

Santiago shrugged. "Laws are for honest men and the rich."

"And you are poor and have a talent for business."

He considered her for a moment in silence. "I wonder how much you really know about this—like maybe that the papers made you sole heir to Gregg's estate. Everything—the house here, land in the Southwest—it would've made you comfortably wealthy for life."

Ill and trembling, Natalie leaned against the fireplace. In her hands the bronze Horus grew cold and heavy.

My God, she wondered desperately, what do I do now? This is mad—completely, totally mad. Here I am, exchanging polite, literate comments with a man who's holding a gun on me. He's going to kill me, and I stand here being witty and civilized—

"I presume you'd like to see the papers, Professor. Are you listening to me, Professor?"

"Yes, I'm listening."

"Good." Santiago's voice was hard with overtones of an unspoken threat. "I dislike being ignored."

"I apologize, but you've handed me rather a shock, you know, and I've had too many lately. I would like very much to see the papers, if I may."

141

Santiago ejected the half-smoked butt from his cigarette holder and ground it out in an ashtray. "I don't like you, Professor, but you've got guts. You'd be easier to work with than Renata. Why, with your nerve and reputation and my talents—"

"For what, Mr. Santiago?"

He laughed. "Any number of things, Professor. You might say 'artistic reproductions!' Well, I guess your police friends have had time to get out of our way, so suppose we start."

Natalie nodded and turned toward the door. "It's cold out," she said suddenly, "hadn't you better let Carla get her coat?"

"Then I'd have two of you to watch—wouldn't I?—and you'd have a better chance to hit me with that damned brass bird. No, Professor, it and she will stay right here. Drop it in that chair, please."

Natalie obeyed without a word. Santiago called Carla to him, ordered her to turn around, and struck her once on the back of the head with the butt of his gun.

"No!" Natalie protested.

"She'll be out for half an hour. By then you and I will be out of sight."

"Will Gregg was killed like that—"

"But not by me, Professor, not by me."

"By whom, then? You do know, don't you?"

Santiago stuck his right hand with the pistol into his jacket pocket. "Yes," he answered, "I know, and if it hadn't been for me the whole thing would've been a waste. I hate useless effort, Professor. It frustrates me to take chances for nothing. I guess that's why the Army and I never got on so well. I refused to jump out of an airplane without damned good reason."

"You were a paratrooper?"

"For exactly six weeks. So you see, I'll have no trouble ending our association, none at all. Especially since I'll have an adequate reason for jumping out of your plane."

"I dare say," Natalie agreed wryly.

Santiago laughed. "It *is* a pity we can't work together, Professor. Truly, it is. Now—please walk ahead of me, and be a lady."

CHAPTER XI

Turk Harrison had driven exactly two blocks when, without comment of any kind, he did a U turn and headed back to the building where they had left Natalie Keith. Jensen, mildly surprised, looked at him in silent demand for explanation.

"My back teeth hurt," Harrison complained, "and that always means trouble."

"My grandmother always complained of her corns"—Jensen smiled in the darkness—"and predicted rain. What are you expecting, other than a dental bill?"

Harrison shrugged. "Thought we'd wait for Mrs. Keith. We aren't in that much of a hurry, are we?"

"No, Sir Launcelot, we aren't."

Harrison grunted, pulled the car around in another U turn, and parked.

"I wouldn't be surprised," Jensen said, "if she's rather annoyed to find us here. She's the independent type, Turk."

"She's also a bad liar."

"Oh?"

"Her gloves were in her jacket pocket. I saw 'em."

Jensen stared at his partner. "Are you sure?"

"Eh-huh. —Look there, Chris."

Jensen looked up to see Natalie and Ramón Santiago coming down the path toward the sidewalk. He was walking slightly behind and to her left, and appeared to be holding her by the elbow. As they came near, Harrison raised his left hand to his face as if to scratch his nose, while Jensen instinctively leaned back into the shadows. Natalie Keith either did not see the car, or ignored it.

"Not very gallant, our Cuban gentleman," Harrison observed, "making the lady walk outside—"

"Two to one he's got a gun in her ribs," Jensen said. "Give

143

him half a block, Turk, and we'll follow on foot. You take the other side of the street in case he crosses."

Harrison nodded, feeling his jaw with an inquisitive forefinger. "I dunno, maybe I'd better not see the dentist. Hate to lose these teeth . . ."

Jensen waited until Harrison had crossed the wide street, then started after Natalie Keith and the man who might or might not have a gun. He had done this before: not too often, to be sure, but often enough to leave him tense and hollow in the middle and dry in the mouth. All of a sudden it had become a matter of bullets and possibly bloodshed and pain for someone, and the shield in his pocket became a heavy thing to bear. If it weren't a war, it was robbery or assault or outright murder. Wherever more than a dozen people got together, sooner or later there was bound to be violence. And sooner or later someone would have to move in and clean things up so it could start all over again somewhere else. People were like that, he guessed.

Natalie Keith walked at a reasonable pace, letting the sound of her own footsteps occupy her attention. If she lived to be a hundred—which at the moment seemed highly unlikely—she would never forget the cadence or the way the cold penetrated the soles of her shoes.

She had thought many times of dying. Once, jockeying a fighter plane across the Rockies, she had come within a few hundred feet of crashing into a mountaintop, and for months had had nightmares in which she saw her own body lying in the wreckage. Now, with Ramón Santiago's little gun prodding her ribs, she relived the experience. Only the mountainside became a back alley and the roar of an exploding plane was reduced to the angry cough of a small-caliber weapon.

Had she been offered a choice, she would have preferred the plane crash. Whatever terror the final seconds of futile struggle might hold, they were—for her—more acceptable than waiting for death at the hand of another human being. A flaw in a machine was an infinitely more reasonable cause for dying than

144

a flaw in a human mind. Death by accident was grim, but death by murder was horrible.

"Slow down," Santiago ordered, and, like a well-trained dog called to heel, she slowed.

"Where are you taking me?"

"You'd like to know, wouldn't you?"

"Yes."

"It's down in a basement, Professor," he answered. "Way down, deep. Like a tomb."

Of course, she thought; it would be. Why is it that we associate tombs with depth? An Anglo-Saxon barrow is above ground level. The Kiowa Indians buried above ground completely. One could even argue that the Mycenaeans, Minoans, and Etruscans . . .

"Hold it," Santiago snapped, "don't be conspicuous. Wait for the light to change."

"Sorry," Natalie said, "I didn't see it. Usually I look before I jaywalk."

Santiago grunted and scowled at the light, and Natalie wondered idly if he were afraid of traffic. The signal changed, and he poked her sharply with the gun as if to remind her who was in command on this march to the tomb.

She remembered her first experience in field archaeology, in Egypt the summer she had met Ben Keith. She had been sent with one of the Arab foremen and a couple of laborers to check a report of a tomb far back in a wadi that sliced from the desert to the valley, and they had found to their astonishment that there actually was a man-made chamber hewn in the rock. Because she was the smallest, and nominally in charge, she had wriggled in to take a closer look and been trapped when a small landslide blocked the entrance behind her. She had lain in pitch blackness for five hours while the Arabs worked to dig her out, and she remembered now the thoughts that had tormented her as the air grew foul and she began to lose consciousness: would they get to her? Had she been abandoned? Would the ghost of the tomb's rightful owner rise in wrath against her? Had he already risen and called down the mountain? It had been hard to lie still, harder still to keep herself awake and alert, and hardest of all to hold down the panic that bubbled up inside her.

It was bubbling again now, and she recognized it in the forlorn hope that to do so would bring it under control. She forced herself to pay complete attention to her surroundings; to concentrate on physical details she would not otherwise have seen. Like the traffic light at the intersection ahead. It was green now, but would almost certainly drop red by the time they reached the corner. It was a busy corner, she saw, counting the cars lined up and waiting. When the light finally turned, there would be a rush of vehicles in both directions. Jaywalking here would be foolish indeed.

The idea that appeared suddenly in her consciousness was absurd, yet she did not dismiss it. If Santiago were really afraid of traffic . . .

She slowed, remarking casually that they would get caught in the middle if they tried to cross now. Beside her Santiago slowed, his attention on the signal. Natalie hesitated until it dropped against them and the first of the cars had passed, then stepped quickly off the curb into traffic.

Santiago shouted angrily and plunged after her. She began to run and got a quarter of the way across before he caught up and grabbed her arm. From the corners of her eyes she saw a pickup truck bearing down from the left, and with all the strength she had she thrust herself forward, forcing him to follow. Then she stopped short, turned sharply to her right, and bumped him as hard as she could with her hip. Santiago, off balance to begin with and thrown farther off by her body check, staggered forward.

The truck hit him dead center, and as the fender grazed her Natalie had a glimpse of the driver's horrified face. Then there was only the shriek of brakes as the earth toppled and lights seemed to explode everywhere. The pavement ripped the skin from her hands as she tumbled, and the hoofs of a thousand horses trampled the breath from her body.

Flayed, bruised, and barely conscious, Natalie lay still and listened as the roaring became a voice that called her name over and over again. She tried to open her eyes, but could not.

"All right, you people," a voice said, "I'm a police officer. Move along—come on, *move!*"

Natalie heard someone groan and realized that it was herself. Nothing hurt, and yet she groaned—

"Nat," someone called, "Nat—can you hear me?"

She tried again and opened her eyes. A familiar face, alternately emerging and receding into a blur, bent close to her own.

"That's better. It's me—Chris Jensen."

"Yes. Chris—"

"Just lie still," he advised gently. "You're all right now."

"Where'd you come from?"

"We were following you. How badly do you hurt?"

She moved her head tentatively, then clenched and opened her fists and moved her feet. "Well," she said, "everything that ought to wiggle, wiggles. I guess I had the wind knocked out of me."

He snorted in mixed anguish and relief. "You did a damned fool thing, Natalie, and I don't know how, but you pulled it off."

"Where's Santiago?— Here, let me sit up. Ow!" She caught her breath sharply and lay back with her eyes closed.

"I thought I told you to lie still," Jensen said severely. "There's an ambulance coming, and you're not to move until it gets here."

"How's Santiago?"

Jensen hesitated, and she marked his uncertainty. "Not so good."

"He's dead, isn't he?"

Jensen nodded, and Natalie closed her eyes as shock and weakness seemed to crush her downward into the earth. "Oh God, oh my God—*what have I done?*"

"It was a brave thing, Natalie," Jensen said, "and the only thing you could have done under the circumstances. It could mean that we have, or soon will have, our murderer."

"It wasn't Ramón Santiago."

"Maybe not, but why did he pull the gun if he wasn't involved? Now lie still, damn it! The ambulance is coming—I can hear it."

147

Natalie lay still, listening to the sirens of the ambulance and two police cars, watching the flashing glare of their red lights on people's faces, and trying to accept the truth that she had killed a man. She—bookworm, scholar, woman of solitary nature—had done the unthinkable.

"Hello," someone said, "look at me, please. How many fingers am I holding up?"

"Two," she answered irritably.

"Move your feet." The white-jacketed newcomer knelt on one knee beside her and felt for her pulse. "Anything in particular hurt?"

"No." She was too weary to be annoyed. "I'm fine—"

The ambulance intern turned on a flashlight and peered into her eyes. Then, quickly and expertly, he took inventory of her cuts and bruises. "Hurt when you take a deep breath? Think you can sit up if we help you?"

Natalie sat up, and was aware for the first time of the size of the crowd that had gathered. Then she stood, leaning on Jensen's shoulder, while the doctor watched critically.

"Better take her along to the hospital, Lieutenant," he ordered. "Be sure someone goes with her who knows what happened. Lady"—he smiled at Natalie for the first time—"you lead a charmed life!"

She thanked him and stifled an impulse to howl. Here she stood, alive and relatively unhurt, having taken one life and put another—Carla Duval's—in considerable danger.

"Chris," she said, "the girl—Carla—"

"It's okay, Nat. Turk's on his way there now. Let's go to the squad car . . . easy does it now . . ."

He helped her into the back seat and got in beside her, thinking that she looked smaller and older than she ought. How much of this, he wondered, was the result of physical, and how much of emotional, shock? She might not be badly hurt, but the hurts she did have were the sort that could cause more simple, old-fashioned pain than a serious wound. Her hands, in particular, were raw.

"What happens now?" she asked suddenly.

"Oh, you'll get a tetanus shot, a good scrub, and maybe some stitches, and I'll get you back looking like King Tut himself."

"I don't mean to me, I mean to the case. When I recognized the Horus—"

"Whoa!" He smiled at her. "Let's wait till you're patched up. And *who,* pray tell, is Horace?"

Giddy, and for no reason she could think of, amused, Natalie laughed. Her own voice sounded strange in her ears. "Chris," she asked, "do you suppose I have a concussion? I feel like the loser in a prize fight—"

"You look kinda like one too," he answered cheerfully. "You were out cold for a couple of minutes, Natalie. In fact, people were beginning to think I was nuts, kneeling there talking to myself."

"Were you facing Mecca?"

He laughed, and she joined him. "I'm not only concussed," she said, trying to stop, "I'm hysterical! My God, Chris—what's wrong with me?"

"You're what's known in the trade as 'all shook up.' You've been rattled right down to the ends of your toes, and this is the usual reaction. If you want to cry, go ahead. I've got wide shoulders."

With a suddenness that bewildered her her unbidden merriment switched to weeping, and she leaned back against the seat while tears streamed down her face. Wisely, she made no effort to stop, and after a few moments felt herself begin to steady. Perhaps he was right; perhaps this was just the reaction to shock.

"This is the Emergency Entrance, Lieutenant!" the driver called out. "Need any help?"

"I don't think so," he answered. "You can make it under your own steam, can't you, Nat?"

"I think so but Chris—about Carla—I tried to tell you earlier—she's hurt. Santiago hit her with his gun, and I'm afraid—"

Jensen nodded and turned to the driver. "Check it, will you, Jake? I'll be inside—let me know right away."

What happened to her next would always, Natalie decided,

have a faintly surrealistic cast in her memory. Her own suit jacket and blouse, torn and soaked with dirty water, gasoline, and her own blood, was taken and replaced by an intern's white tunic. Her temperature, pulse, respiration, and blood pressure were recorded; she was given a tetanus shot, X rayed, examined by what seemed to be a full regiment of doctors, and finally abandoned in a small room that would have done credit to a medieval ascetic. There, lying in solitude and quiet on a sparsely padded examining table, she tried hard to organize her thoughts.

Her head had begun to ache at some point, and somehow she had not quite the courage to look at her hands. Instead she lay, shivering spasmodically, and forced her tense body to relax. Strangely, her chronic fear of hospitals seemed to have vanished.

A nurse appeared, carrying a blanket that she spread over her. "How are we?" she asked.

"We," Natalie answered, half amused and half exasperated, "seem to be about as well as can be expected, but we'd appreciate an aspirin or two."

The nurse, who had a sense of humor, laughed softly. "The doctor will be with you in a moment. He's reading your X rays."

"Sounds like a proclamation of doom. Will I make the best-seller list?"

"I doubt it. You were terribly lucky—"

Natalie's mirth faded again as it had in the police car, leaving her depressed and frightened. "I killed a man," she said before she could stop herself, "is that considered lucky?"

"I understand"—the nurse nodded sympathetically and Natalie had an impulse to strike her—"but it was an accident. A detective saw the whole thing. . . . Here's the doctor."

"Hello, Natalie." He filled the door with his bulk. "This seems to be your day with the Hollanders."

"Mike!" she said, grateful for his presence, "how do I rate an assistant chief of staff?"

"You don't." He handed her chart to the nurse. "I was in the house checking a post-op patient when I saw your name on

150

the emergency admission list, and here I am. Tell me, aren't you a little old for bullfighting?"

"I'll get the dressing cart," the nurse announced tactfully, and left.

Natalie felt herself begin to cry again, and it angered her. Mike Hollander ignored her.

"I've spoken to Lieutenant Jensen," he said, starting his examination. "You're really incredible, Nat. One of these days your luck will run out. This is the dullest set of X rays I've read in days."

"Anything broken?"

"Eh-huh. You've got two hundred bones in your carcass, give or take a few, any one of which you could have pulverized, and what do you break? The first and second metacarpals of your right hand."

The nurse came back with the dressing cart, and helped Mike Hollander as he started to work, rapidly and without haste, cleaning and dressing Natalie's assorted cuts and abrasions. She lay still, eyes closed, and stubbornly determined not to make a sound.

"From the variety of faces you're making," he said, "I gather I'm hurting you."

Natalie swore extensively in Greek.

"Well, what do you expect?" he demanded, "you've got half the road under your hide."

"Oh, shut up!"

"The worst is over, old girl," he comforted gruffly. "All that's left is fixing the hand, and I'll give you a shot for that. If you hadn't lost so much skin I'd put you in a cast. As it is, I'll have to splint you. I suppose you'll buck like a steer with its tail in the gate if I suggest a day or two in this antiseptic motel."

"You suppose right." Natalie winced at the needle's merciful bite.

"Ah me, what's that TV medic got that I haven't?"

"Do you really want to know?"

He smiled and moved her hand experimentally. "I've already told Lieutenant Whatshisname he can have you back. . . . Feel that?"

"A little."

He reached for the hypodermic. "Want more?"

"No, it's all right. But I would like a couple of aspirin."

"Ehm?— Oh, sure. I'll give you something later."

Natalie caught the nurse's eye and grinned. "Would you care to bet on that?"

Mike Hollander looked up with a faintly puzzled expression. "What goes on?"

The nurse, struggling with her dignity, cleared her throat loudly. Natalie contrived to look totally innocent. He made a face and stared at her.

"Now don't tell me," he said, "that you believe that slander about aspirin being so hard to get in hospitals!"

"And safety pins," Natalie added, "don't forget safety pins."

He groaned, and the nurse, stretched beyond the limits of self-discipline, giggled. For the rest of the time he worked over Natalie Keith, Doctor Hollander maintained as dignified a silence as he could.

"There," he said finally, adjusting her sling, "you know, Natalie, I'd hate to see you after a serious accident. They'd probably ask you to play the Palace with a troupe of trained seals. You can go now."

"'And never darken your door again.'" Natalie balanced on the edge of the table and stared down at her bandaged hands.

"They're going to stiffen up and hurt like hell," he warned, "in fact, you'll be pretty sore all over. Better plan to have someone stay with you, because you won't be doing much for a week or so."

"I'll manage, Mike."

"Knowing you, I'm sure you will. I want to see you Saturday at the office. Come for lunch and we'll make it a social call."

She agreed and stood up, aware of the tug of the sling at the back of her neck. Mike Hollander walked with her through the corridors to the waiting room, where Jensen and Turk Harrison sat in deep conversation.

"One of you care to take delivery on a slightly damaged archaeologist?" he asked.

Jensen looked up, saw her, and grinned. "I sure would! How do you feel, Nat?"

"I have a headache," she announced, "and I'd like an aspirin."

Turk Harrison reached into his pocket and produced a box. "Here, hold these while I get you some water."

She took the box awkwardly in her left hand and turned a withering look on Mike Hollander. "Chris," she asked, "how's Carla Duval?"

"She's been admitted here," he answered, "but I haven't seen her. There's a Doctor McIvor with her."

"Neurosurgeon," Mike Hollander told them, "one of the best in the country."

"Several things have happened in the past two hours, Natalie," Jensen went on. "We'll talk in the car, if you feel up to it."

Natalie swallowed her long-sought aspirin and handed the empty paper cup to Mike Hollander. "Thanks for the patch-up, Mike. I'll see you Saturday. Give my regards to Peg."

He waved a casual good-by and watched her go, looking like a slightly battered gamecock between two eagles.

It was cold outside, and Jensen paused long enough to drape his jacket around her shoulders. Harrison brought the car up to the entrance, and she sat between the two men on the front seat. It was warm inside, and she was grateful.

"How do you feel?" Jensen asked after a moment.

"Mentally, alert and reasonable. Physically—I've begun to find muscles I'd forgotten I had! Now—what's been happening?"

"Plenty! To begin, Ramón Santiago is really one Dave Santos, who's wanted in New York, Pittsburgh, and points west for paper hanging."

"For how much?"

"Paper hanging," Jensen explained, "in plain English, passing bad checks. He's also done time for forgery."

"The only thing Cuban about him," Harrison added, "was his cigar."

"There was a hotel key in his pocket," Jensen went on, "and we found Doctor Gregg's 'Personal' file in the room. The missing draft of the codicil was there, and, just to make it interesting, a

153

stack of other papers apparently—but only apparently—in Gregg's handwriting."

In the darkness Natalie wrinkled her brow. "Santiago—or Santos, I mean—said I was named in the codicil. It isn't true, is it?"

"Yes," Jensen answered, "though some of the other papers seemed to alter it in favor of someone else."

"How did Santos get hold of the file in the first place?" Natalie asked. "For that matter, how did Will's bronze Horus get to Renata Duval's apartment? And how did Renata get mixed up with a man like Santos?"

"You tell me," Jensen said gloomily.

"We're going to Will's house, aren't we?" she asked.

"Yes. The answers are there, Natalie, I'm sure of it."

"So'm I." She sighed. "The problem is—where?"

CHAPTER XII

Back again in Will Gregg's library, Natalie sat nursing a cup of coffee that a policeman had produced seemingly from nowhere, and waiting for Jensen and Harrison to join her. Mike Hollander's prediction that she would be "sore as hell" was proving dismally true. Still, she thought, gingerly lifting her cup with a left hand, which was awkward even under normal conditions, she had been unbelievably lucky.

The logic of her own thoughts brought her abruptly face to face with the truth that she had caused the death of Ramón Santiago. Or, as might be, Dave Santos. The reckless act that had taken his life began to haunt her. She could have waited: Jensen had been close behind all the time, and would have intervened before Santos could have harmed her.

But she had not waited, and there was no running from her ultimate responsibility for his death. Now, safe and reasonably comfortable, she tried to remember exactly what had happened and found that she could not. All she could recall was his scream as it merged with the shriek of brakes, and her own sensations of being struck and of falling. All reason, all emotion, had vanished, leaving only dreamlike impressions with neither background nor foreground to lend them reality.

"Are you asleep?" Jensen asked gently, coming into the room.

"No, just thinking."

"About Santos?"

"Yes."

He came over and leaned against the table near her. "Cops don't make good preachers, Natalie, but one word of advice—forget the whole thing as quickly as you can."

"I've already begun to. I can't even remember what I did."

"Good. Accept it as one of the Almighty's subtler blessings.

Look, I've had to kill people too, and brooding doesn't help. It doesn't help at all. As for Santos, anyone has the right to kill in self-defense."

"I know that, Chris. It's just—I'm not a violent person by nature."

He offered her a cigarette and she took it. "Here I go sounding cynical again, but I don't believe there's any such thing as a nonviolent human being. Most of us, by a happy combination of luck and self-discipline, never have to use it, but the capacity is there. We're born with it."

"You're probably right, Chris, but the shock lingers."

"It sure does."

Turk Harrison arrived looking morose and unhappy. "I just spoke to Charlie," he said. "New Orleans reports no passenger named Duval on the two-thirty A.M. plane last Thursday. They also say they have no Marvin Endicot listed, though they do have a Melvin and two Martins. They're checking it out."

Jensen nodded silently, and Natalie saw the muscles at the angle of his jaw pull into hard knots under the skin.

"The captain," Harrison went on, "also just happened to mention that maybe you could use Lieutenant Cummings to help."

"The hell he did!"

"I'm sorry, Chris, but it doesn't look good, our having lost the Duval woman."

"'We' didn't lose her, Turk; *I* did, all by myself. Did he say when Cummings would take over?"

"No, but if I know the Boy, it won't be until tomorrow morning."

Jensen tossed an empty matchbook into a wastebasket and fumbled in his pocket for another. "Then we still have time to talk, just talk, and maybe get this thing organized. By the way, are you checking the New Orleans hospitals for a patient matching what we know of Duval's sister?"

Harrison nodded and handed Jensen a lighter. "There's something else, Chris. One of the witnesses to the accident was a reporter who recognized the professor, so the squeeze is on.

156

Captain Hayes gave out a statement that Santos tried to snatch her purse and was run down while trying to escape."

"That won't satisfy anyone for long."

"No," Harrison agreed, "unless the press is off on a sweet-and-innocent kick. I just thought I'd warn you."

Natalie sat, watching and listening, and realized suddenly and with a sense of outrage that, however well and intelligently Jensen had handled things so far, he was being replaced.

"I don't understand this, Chris," she protested. "Is Renata that important? I'm sure she told you everything she knows about Will."

"She probably has," he agreed, "but she *is* 'that important,' Natalie. For one thing, we've got to know about her relationship to Dave Santos. For instance, how did he come by Doctor Gregg's papers?"

"Yeah," Harrison added, "and how did that bronze bird get into Duval's apartment?"

"Well"—Natalie tried desperately to think—"as I told you, I noticed it needed treatment. Will might've asked Renata to drop it off at the museum for him."

"But you said you didn't mention that to Doctor Gregg—"

"I know, Chris, but Will saw me looking at the Horus, and he might have noticed its condition for himself. There were times when I thought he could read my mind."

"Possible," Jensen conceded, "but what about the papers? How did Santos get them from Duval?"

"How did he come to know Duval in the first place?" Harrison asked.

"Renata," Natalie answered, "has a wide and weird circle of acquaintance. If this man was pretending to be Cuban, Renata might well have taken him under her wing."

"Carla Duval said that Santos's—alias Santiago's—father had been a friend of her father. I assume"—Harrison scowled—"that that would make her father Renata's brother—"

"We're getting ahead of ourselves," Jensen broke in. "I don't think Duval's relationship to the girl is as important right now as a theory on how Santos got the Gregg papers. Can you shed any light, Natalie?"

"I'm not sure. I do remember asking him about it, and all he said was, 'I'm a businessman who hates to pass up an opportunity,' or words to that effect."

Jensen looked hard at her and she recognized the symptoms of rapid thought. "That suggests," he began, "that Santos was snooping, found the papers, and took them. But when?"

Harrison rubbed his chin, which was showing signs of a dark beard. "I'll bet he found 'em after we called Duval and had her come to the Gregg house. He could've heard about the killing on the radio, and just gone fishing for anything he could find."

"I'll buy it as a working theory, Turk. How about you, Nat?"

She nodded but said nothing.

"Okay," Jensen went on, "one more item to consider. Now—suppose we take time to find out what we do and do not know about this whole affair."

"Not much, for my money," Natalie sighed. "I'm confused, and I don't think it's the crack on the head, either."

"No," Jensen agreed, "it isn't. Partly, the trouble is that there are three separate and distinct versions possible—namely, yours, Turk's, and mine. Of these, I think yours and mine are the more important."

"Thanks!" Harrison grinned at him.

"Think nothing of it, old man. And, since we're in a hurry, we'll dispense with democracy completely. Natalie, tell us exactly what went on in your head from the moment the three of us went to Duval's apartment."

"You won't believe it," she said, "but I'm not entirely sure."

"Try," he urged, "start anywhere."

She shrugged one shoulder. "I remember getting bored listening to you and Santiago being polite to each other, and that I started woolgathering. As soon as I saw the Horus on the mantel, I knew it wasn't like the rest of the junk."

"Did you recognize it?"

"It would sound great if I could say I did, Chris, but I didn't. I just knew I wanted to see it again, closer. I should've told you, I know, but I was afraid you'd laugh at me."

"I might have," he admitted. "Go on, please, Nat."

"Well, I invented that silly story about my gloves and went back. I asked Carla to check Renata's desk and briefcase for an envelope addressed to Will's attorney, and went into the living room to look at the Horus. It's the one from Will's collection, Chris, no doubt about it."

"Was Santos there?"

"He came in while I was looking at the hawk. He had followed us out, and he was as cold as ice when he admitted it. I've never been so frightened in my life. It was like talking to a—to a snake."

"I can imagine. Did he say anything about Doctor Gregg?"

"He said he didn't kill him," she answered, "and he knew about the codicil. He told me everything about it."

"Where was he taking you when we caught up?"

She looked at him, grateful for his evasion of fact. "To a room in a basement somewhere. He was going to show me the papers, and then engineer my demise in a plane crash."

Harrison whistled through his teeth and stared at her.

"Natalie"—Jensen came to stand before her—"if you have any feelings about what happened to Santos, that should wipe them out."

"I know what the law allows," she said wearily, "it allows me to take a life to save my own. But don't you see, Chris? There've been two lives lost already, and Carla Duval hurt God knows how badly, and we don't know why. We know less about this thing now than we did a week ago."

Jensen's eyebrows hunched thoughtfully together. "Maybe, and maybe not. There are four separate problems here, and there may be four separate answers. Look at it this way: one —who took the hawk? Two—who took the papers? Three— who killed Doctor Gregg? Four—there has to be four, you know, or the others don't mean much—are one and two connected to three?"

"Wouldn't they have to be?"

"Probably, yes. Not impossibly, no. The thief might've come in and found Doctor Gregg already dead."

"Sure," she said, "and I might wander into the bank at midnight and find the vault wide open."

He smiled. "I won't beat it to death, but the point is, we can assume nothing. Anyhow, let's consider our possibilities." He laid four pieces of paper on the table, each with a different question written on it. "Now—have you any answers, Natalie?"

"No, just a silly question. Why should anyone steal a not-very-unusual bronze of no intrinsic value and precious little artistic merit? Granted, it's impressively old—at least to a layman—but it's worth no more than the metal it contains. One look at that apartment tells you Renata isn't interested in real antiques."

"You seem convinced that Duval took the hawk. Why?"

"Because no one else could have, except Peter, who didn't."

"That's logical. In other words, you believe that Duval came back after you'd had lunch with Doctor Gregg, picked up the papers to do at home, and also took the hawk, with the intention of delivering it to the museum later on."

She nodded.

Harrison broke a long silence. "Okay, how did Santos get into the picture?"

Natalie glared at him. "I was afraid you'd ask that, Turk."

Jensen, who had been contemplating his four scraps of paper, groaned and passed his hands over his face. "This is the damnedest mess I've ever seen!"

"It's a beaut, it is," Harrison agreed.

Natalie also turned her attention to the four pieces of paper, and a leaden silence filled the room. In her tiredness, in the pain that increased steadily as shock and anesthetic wore off, she found herself blocked and baffled, however she tried to use her mind. Just beyond reach was an idea, and in determined defiance of an urgent need to sleep she snatched at it.

"I think we've got a fifth possibility."

"So do I," Jensen agreed, "the classic 'person or persons unknown' in whose being Santos, Duval, and our killer find their connection."

"You," she accused, "sound like some demonic theologian explaining an article of faith."

"What do you think I feel like?"

160

"I'm waiting for nominations," Harrison said. "Who is Mr. X?"

"All right, gentlemen, I submit the name of Miss Hernandes, whose father once helped Will Gregg out of trouble in South America."

"Hear! Hear!" Jensen said. "But why, Natalie?"

"Because she's an unknown quantity. At least, she is to me."

"I hate to sound stupid," Harrison argued, "but what about a motive?"

"Also a classic," Jensen theorized, "blackmail. She knows that Doctor Gregg has been in prison, and threatens to tell the University authorities. He pays until he can't any more and then"—he snapped his fingers, making Natalie start sharply and painfully—"there's a scene, Hernandes loses her temper, and Doctor Gregg loses his life. When she realizes what she's done, she takes his papers and runs to Dave Santos to forge a new codicil naming her sole heir instead of Natalie. How's that?"

"Chris," she said, "you ought to write. Then, maybe, you could also unravel the connection between Santos and Renata Duval."

"*Touché!*" Jensen smiled. "I'd forgotten that."

"Actually," Harrison admitted, "it's not as far out as it sounds. We've come across wilder ones."

"I don't doubt it." She reached gingerly for a cigarette. "On second thought, it's the Hernandes connection that's farfetched. I'm just talking to keep myself conscious at this point."

Jensen, who had been silent for some time, got up and walked to the windows. "We all are, Natalie. Maybe it's a good thing Cummings is taking over. I've made one hell of a botch."

"I don't think so," Natalie said, "and I'm rather an 'interested party,' after all."

"Thanks"—Jensen's back was still toward them—"but I'm the one who let Duval fly off and disappear. I never even ordered an investigation. I never even checked on her relationship to Carla."

"Aunt and niece," Natalie answered, "though there's a strong resemblance between them. I assume Carla is a brother's child,

161

or her name would be different. I don't know Renata at all, personally," she added.

"Over the Alps lies Italy," Harrison observed, "but is it worth the climb?"

Jensen started to speak, but the sound of loud voices in the hall prevented him.

"Hey," someone shouted, "you can't go in there—"

Someone else answered in a low rumble, and the library doors opened abruptly.

"Ah" a deep voice said, "you *are* here—"

Natalie turned as quickly as she could and saw Edward Ken in the doorway, ignoring the efforts at his removal being made by a small policeman. She stared at him as at a stranger.

"I've been looking all over this city for you," he told her as he came into the room. "Those idiots at the hospital refused to tell me where you were, and the police were no more helpful."

"Edward, may I introduce Lieutenant Jensen and Sergeant Harrison—"

"Ken"—he offered his hand—"Edward Ken, department of anthropology. Pleasure to meet you both."

Jensen, obviously confused, acknowledged the compliment and looked helplessly to Natalie for some sort of explanation.

"Edward," she began tentatively, "I don't suppose you care to explain how—or why—you're here—"

"I heard about the accident on the radio." He looked at her with deep concern in his sea-colored eyes. "Are you all right, Natalie? Surely you aren't planning to work with your hands like that—"

"I hadn't thought that far ahead," she confessed. "Do you mean to tell me the news is out at this hour? By the way, what time is it?"

"Three forty-seven," Jensen answered, looking at his watch. "Those boys work fast, especially when you don't want 'em to. Look here, why don't you go home and get some rest? I need you, but I also want you in reasonably good shape."

"An excellent idea, Lieutenant. I'm taking her home with me."

162

"Now look here, you two—"

"Well, you obviously can't fend for yourself with one arm broken and the other sprained, or whatever it is—"

"It'll be tricky," she conceded, "but if I stop moving now, I'll be stuck for days. I have my second wind, and I'd like to see this thing through. After all, I'm the one who killed Santos—"

Edward Ken's face went white, and he turned to Jensen.

"She had no choice, Doctor Ken," he explained. "Santos had a gun in her back. All right, Nat, hang on a while longer. But as soon as we reach a stopping point I personally will deliver you to Doctor Ken's address."

"Fair enough." She nodded.

Ken stuffed his hands into his jacket pockets. "Look, just what *is* going on here? Is this latest thing connected with Will Gregg's death?"

Jensen nodded. "But not for public consumption. At least, not yet."

"Shades of E. Phillips Oppenheim—"

"It was more like Mickey Spillane for a while." Natalie grinned at Turk Harrison.

"Is there danger?"

"Yes," Jensen answered, "but I doubt if it's to Natalie. We're dealing with a murderer, Doctor Ken, and they're always dangerous."

Sobered but not intimidated, Edward Ken nodded and stood straight. "Anything I can do to help?"

"As a matter of fact, yes. Do you have a car?"

"Of a sort—"

"Then you can drive Sergeant Harrison to the city morgue to pick up Santos's personal effects. On the way you might stop at police headquarters so he can leave off these notes—"

Startled, Natalie looked at him, wondering why he should send both men off on what she sensed was a wild goose chase. It seemed a useless errand, and yet this was not a man given to meaningless gestures.

Jensen collected his five sheets of paper from the table, arranged them carefully with some others from his notebook, and reached for the stapler that stood beside the neat pile of oddments from Will Gregg's desk. He pressed firmly on the handle, then swore.

"I forgot," he said, "this unspeakable thing is jammed."

Edward Ken reached out and took it from him. "There's a trick with these things," he said, turning it upside down. "Will's so-called secretary showed me once. You push this lever —like this—and it opens out so you can get at the muzzle. Ah-ha! There she goes—see?"

The stapler unfolded suddenly and swung like a pendulum from its rear hinge. Ken turned it over and held it out, and the top part fell back so that it formed a straight, and, in this position, rigid tool rather more than a foot long and with a sharp-cornered, square end pointing upward toward the ceiling. Natalie, watching, went cold with sudden recognition.

Jensen too reacted to the sight of the unfolded stapler. Slowly, like a man reaching for a rare butterfly that has alighted on his porch rail, he took the tool from Ken's hand, hefted it, and studied it for a brief, intent moment.

"No," Natalie said tonelessly, "it couldn't be—"

"Turk"—Jensen's voice was glacial—"take this to the lab and stay with it until the report is in. I don't care *who* you wake up. Have it checked for blood type, skin, and hair. There's something jamming this, and my guess is it's human tissue."

Edward Ken sat down and looked at Natalie in bewilderment. But the most she could do was shake her head in inarticulate protest against a truth suddenly glaringly evident.

"My God," Ken said, "you mean *that thing*— But that's horrible!"

CHAPTER XIII

What Edward Ken, student of humanity, had instinctively known and titled horror settled over the library with a heavy and silent presence. Turk Harrison left quickly and unobtrusively while Jensen, who had not moved from his place at the table, sat with his notebook open as if reading. But the anthropologist, watchful and observant, knew that he did not see what he stared at, and guessed that his mind was elsewhere.

Across the table from him Natalie Keith sat with her eyes closed and her head tipped and resting on the chair back. Her face, drawn and shadowed, was unexpressive, but her whole being bespoke exhaustion of body and spirit. Edward Ken, studying her with the deep concern of friendship, marveled that she had been able to take as much as she had already, and wondered how near she was to her limits.

"Lieutenant," he said quietly.

Jensen looked up blankly, then recollected him. "Yes?"

"I'm going out to get you and Natalie something to eat."

"I'm not hungry," she said, "but thanks anyhow."

"I think he's right, Nat." Jensen spoke gently. "Even if you can't eat, a little hot coffee might help. Bring me the receipt, sir, and we'll let City Hall do the honors."

Edward Ken said something that crackled like heat lightning. "A Japanese word," he explained, "which is never translated for ladies, and which expresses my opinion of that last sentiment. Damn it, Will Gregg was a friend of mine too!"

Natalie heard him go and opened her eyes. "One meets so few good people, and I seem to know so many—" She said no more, letting the statement drift like a fragment of thought made audible.

"They come in bunches," Jensen added, "in unexpected places."

165

"Will was best man when Edward and Michi were married," she went on, "and he was going to return the compliment for us."

Jensen looked at her, not knowing what to say, but wanting to reassure her.

She smiled at him. "I'm all right, Chris, just in a trough between two waves. I'll revive in a little."

"Sure. Are you hurting badly?"

"Just a little above nuisance level."

He folded his notebook and looked at his watch. "I've got to call and see if there's anything from New Orleans. Will you be all right alone?"

"I won't move," she answered, only half in jest. "I promise."

"Cigarette?"

"Thanks. Mine disappeared with my jacket. —Lord, I make a clumsy southpaw!"

"I've seen better," he agreed as he lit her cigarette. "I won't be long."

Alone, Natalie smoked slowly and determinedly, concentrating her attention on the act itself and her response to it. She studied the cigarette, aware of its precision of form and the sharp division between its burned and unburned halves, and then shifted her attention to her own battered hand.

It's someone else's, she thought, some other woman whose life got all mixed up and who killed a man she didn't even know. This can't be happening to me—it can't!

The cigarette burned dangerously low, and she leaned forward to reach an ashtray. The effort caused her to feel as if every muscle in her back and shoulder had torn loose. She hesitated a moment and leaned back slowly, resting against the chair. The things that had happened were real, and like it or not, they had happened to her.

Caught between the need to know the truth and a lashing desire to deny it, Natalie felt herself beginning to lose control. Only her physical distress bound her to reality, and she turned willingly to it, at once embracing and resting upon it. At least pain was something she knew and could understand; in a world bereft of order, this at least was predictable and reliable.

166

In another time and in another nation she would have been proud to have avenged her dead. But the violent death of Dave Santos would not bring back Will Gregg: murdered good could not be restored by slaughtered evil, though an hundred be offered for one. Nay, though a thousand be offered for one. Electra, avenging Agamemnon, accomplished nothing more than the compounding of Clytemnestra's crime.

A sound close at hand caused her to pull taut and open her eyes. Both Jensen and Edward Ken had returned and were holding a whispered conference at the far end of the long table.

"Planning to rob a bank?" she asked politely.

Jensen grinned, but Ken looked only slightly more than usually Mephisophelean. "I told you she never needs more than fifteen minutes' sleep."

Jensen bowed. "Sir, I salute your superior wisdom!"

"What are you two talking about?" she demanded. "I wasn't asleep."

"Well then," Ken teased, "you were deep enough in thought to get the bends from coming up too fast. We've been here for ten minutes, and you were far gone when we arrived."

She chose to ignore him. "I'm hungry. What did you manage to find?"

"Toasted bat's wings and mosquito tongues."

She got unsteadily to her feet. "I'll bet you forgot the mustard."

"You're nuts," Jensen said, "both of you."

"Oh, you should see us at faculty meetings, Lieutenant. I've known Dean Durwent to turn purple if we so much as looked at one another."

"By the way," Jensen asked, "how is the dean? I've been busily ignoring him."

"Ah"—the anthropologist waggled a forefinger at him—"but he hasn't forgotten you, old man, not a whit. He spent most of Monday grumbling about professors who fly airplanes and detectives who encourage that sort of thing."

Natalie laughed.

"Laugh if you must, madam, but I had to listen to him all afternoon."

"I'm sorry, Edward, but I had a fleeting vision of his expression when he learned where I was."

"It was a dilly."

"I'll bet!" She consulted the calendar on the wall by Will Gregg's abandoned desk. "Was that only Monday, and is this just Wednesday?"

"No," Jensen answered, "it's Thursday now."

Sobered, Natalie stood for a moment leaning against the filing cabinet. A week ago to the hour she had stood in this room, trying to understand that Will Gregg was dead, and still she could not wholly believe it. Would she ever, she wondered?

"Natalie?" Jensen asked.

"Nothing, Chris," she answered, "just wondering how seven days can seem longer than seven years."

"Come eat your steak, Natalie," Edward Ken urged. "The paradox can wait upon the morrow, but the meat grows cold."

Somehow, probably by using every ounce of his professional persuasiveness and personal charm, Edward Ken had managed to get steak sandwiches that were not only large but edible. Even the coffee, Natalie admitted grudgingly, tasted good.

"Odd time of day for a picnic," Jensen observed, licking his fingers unashamedly, "but satisfying."

"Highly," Natalie agreed. "Edward, you amaze me."

"I startle my wife sometimes too, but it's uncanny what one can accomplish when one knows the night watchman at the University cafeteria."

"You didn't!" she said.

"I did. We're going to have a very puzzled dietician in the morning."

"There are, sir," Jensen told him severely, "laws against larceny."

Ken stroked his beard, "I thought of that, so—making use of my extensive knowledge of witchcraft, I left little cat tracks all over the place."

Natalie, wearing a pained expression, wondered aloud if it were the hour or the company. Jensen was about to reply when Turk Harrison walked in and, without comment, handed him

168

an envelope. He read the contents slowly, then tucked it inside his notebook.

"The results of all tests were positive," he reported quietly. "Incredible as it sounds, Doctor Gregg was killed with that stapling machine. Now all we have to do is figure out by whom—"

"What about fingerprints?" Edward Ken asked.

Jensen shook his head. "Too many people have handled the thing since last week, including yours obediently."

"Chris," Natalie asked suddenly, "are they *sure?* I mean, it's such a—such an unlikely thing for a murder weapon."

"They're sure," he answered.

"But who in the world—there's a paper knife right on the desk. Why use a stapling machine?"

"You tell me." He smiled lopsidedly at her. "In fact, I'd like suggestions from all of you."

"I didn't even know the fool thing opened up," Harrison volunteered.

"I did," Natalie said. "How come you knew, Edward?"

He shrugged. "Some secretary showed me. It might have been that gem of Will's, or it might've been Kate at the office. I'm not sure. It might even have been my wife. She's an endless source of odd and peculiar knowledge."

"Speaking of Duval," Harrison said, "the New Orleans police report that the other Endicot leads dried up. No birth certificate was ever issued there for a Renata Duval, either, although of course that might be her married name."

"But she isn't," Natalie interrupted, "unless—"

"You're thinking of Santos," Jensen said.

"I don't know what I'm thinking, Chris. This whole thing is beyond me."

"Me too," Edward Ken admitted. "If there's nothing I can do, Lieutenant, I might as well get out of the way. Here's my address, so you can deliver Natalie."

"You make me sound like a side of beef."

"No," he said seriously, "ground hamburger."

She stared at him. "Great Caesar's ghost, I forgot Linda Harper! She's at my apartment, sick. Could you call her, Edward, and tell her I'm not coming home? I'd scare her to death coming in like this."

"Probably," he agreed too readily for her liking. "You've an elegant black eye taking shape, you know—"

"No, I didn't."

"It's quite a mouse, Professor," Turk Harrison agreed.

Natalie began to laugh, and Jensen shot a worried look at Edward Ken. She saw, and this too amused her.

"Don't worry, Chris," she said, "I'm not hysterical again. But if I don't laugh, I'll cry. You've got to admit that this *is* an improbable situation for a middle-aged female professor!"

"And you," Edward Ken glowered at her, "are an improbable female professor, middle-aged or not. Thursday is Michi's day to volunteer at the hospital, so I'll ask her to stop by and reorganize Miss Harper for you."

He left, and Natalie used the diversion to tighten her control. Turk Harrison offered her a cigarette, lit it, and spent several moments looking for a clean ashtray.

"I don't know how you do it, Mrs. Keith," he said admiringly. "I wish I had your nerves."

"It gets harder each time, Turk." She smiled with one side of her mouth pulling further up than the other. "Let's hope I don't need to try again—I may become a chain smoker if I do!"

"Something just occurred to me." Jensen spoke thoughtfully, obviously not having heard their conversation. "Natalie, do you recall what you said and did the first time I found that the stapler was jammed?"

"Good heavens, Chris, that was a week ago—"

"A while ago," he chided, "you were asking if it was 'only a week ago.'"

"Well, sure, but—"

"I remember," he went on, "you asked me to give you the stapler because you thought you could fix it. What had you in mind?"

She stared at him, and her face went slowly and totally blank. "I was going to open it out and run a paper clip up into the barrel."

"And do you remember what Doctor Ken said when he actually did open it?"

"Yes," she answered tonelessly, "he said he knew a trick that Renata had taught him. But he qualified that later, Chris. He said it might've been Kate—"

"Where did you learn the same trick?"

She felt the pressure of his questions almost as a physical force, and covered her face with her free hand as if to shut him away from her awareness.

"Think, Natalie," he urged, "it's important."

"Take it easy, Chris," Harrison countered, "lay off—"

"I saw Jeanne, our secretary, do it," Natalie managed to answer.

"A secretary," Jensen repeated, "a woman—"

"Oh, for crying out loud!" Harrison snorted, "this isn't a woman's killing!"

"Murder*ers* have sexes, Turk," Jensen snapped, "but murders don't. Doesn't either of you see what I'm driving at?"

"Sure," Harrison answered, not the least intimidated, "the killer could've been a woman. But what woman, and why?"

"Consider, if you will," Jensen proposed, "what Natalie said about the Hernandes woman's being a possible suspect."

"Oh, come off it!" Harrison jammed his hands into his trouser pockets. "That's reaching pretty far for a— Holy smoke, I'd forgotten this—"

He withdrew his right hand and offered Jensen a long brown envelope. "Wilcox brought this into the lab," he apologized. "It arrived this afternoon, and he thought you might want it. I forgot it completely, Chris. Sorry—"

Jensen took the envelope and frowned. " 'Embassy of ———' now what the hell—"

"The transcripts of Will's trial," Natalie said. "They promised to send them—remember?"

"The long arm of coincidence. Remind me never to belittle it again."

He tore off the end of the envelope and pulled out a thick fold of papers. Natalie came and stood beside him, and he spread them out on the table.

"They forgot to translate," she said unhappily. "Does either of your read Spanish?"

"No," Jensen said, shuffling the papers, "how about you?"

"Latin, Greek, and the hieroglyphs with the help of a good diction— Hey, turn that back, will you?"

"Why?"

"That clipping, the one with the two photographs. One looked familiar—yes, that's it. Who does it remind you of?"

"Absolutely no one. Sorry—"

"Wait a minute," Turk Harrison said, "it does look familiar —but who?"

The pictures were of two men; two formal portraits united in one frame. One was Will Gregg, and Natalie felt a jab of grief at the sight of his familiar face. The other bore the legend "Alfonso Hernandes." It was to this that she called attention.

"Look hard, Turk," she urged, "imagine him without the mustache—and with longer hair and a soft collar."

Harrison bit his lip and scowled. "Sorry, it won't come. But it does remind me of someone."

Natalie's eyes narrowed. "Glasses, sometimes wears glasses—"

"The Duval woman!"

"Exactly."

"Are you trying to suggest," Jensen demanded, staring at them, "that *this* is Renata Duval—"

"No," Natalie answered, "but I am suggesting that Renata looks enough like Alfonso Hernandes to be his daughter."

"That's torn it!" Jensen fumbled with a new pack of cigarettes.

"Remember," Natalie said gently, "you only saw her for a moment."

"Granted," he answered, bridling at the incredible but completely logical conclusion to which she was leading him, "but the Hernandes girl was last known to be living in Texas."

"And Renata claims to come from New Orleans, conveniently across the Gulf of Mexico. And the ages tally. Isn't it enough for a working theory?"

"Except that it's impossible, yes."

"Heinrich Schliemann took poems written some three thou-

172

sand years before his own birth and used them to locate Troy and Mycenae."

"That's archaeology, not police work."

"And is your work so much less logical or scientific than mine?"

He groaned and lit a cigarette. "Natalie, are you seriously proposing that Renata Duval and the Hernandes woman are one and the same?"

"Exactly. Can you disprove it?"

"No," he admitted, "as far as interpreting circumstantial evidence goes, you've been downright brilliant. But it's—it's incredible."

"So were Troy and Mycenae. So was Tutankhamen. So— to change fields—was the microbe theory—"

Jensen shrugged and turned away. "All right," he said, starting to pace, "since we've nothing else to work on, I'll take option on your idea. What about motive?"

"I'm an archaeologist, not a psychologist."

"Look at it this way, Chris," Turk Harrison began with plodding logic, "Duval's done the following: she lied about her reason for leaving town, and she lied about her destination. She was also apparently involved in an attempt to forge a codicil to Gregg's will. You yourself talked about blackmail a while back, you know."

"You're as bad as Natalie," Jensen growled.

"Well, I don't know how *she* feels about that, but I take it as a compliment."

Jensen exhaled a lungful of smoke and turned to face them. "Okay," he challenged, "now what?"

"Find Duval-Hernandes," Natalie said.

He grinned spitefully at her. "Got any three-thousand-year-old guidebooks?"

"No," she answered, "just a couple of clichés. First—the only thing you can't hide is a hole in the ground. Second—the best place to hide something is in plain sight."

"Which being interpreted, meaneth that Duval is still in town."

She nodded.

173

"Where?"

"I was afraid you'd ask that," she said with a wry grin.

"You knew damned well I would."

"Ey-yuh. Now *think*, Chris. What did Renata say when you asked her to come into this room?"

"She said she couldn't because she was a 'sensitive.'"

"And what did you say?"

"I asked her if she meant she was a medium."

"Splendid! Now we're getting somewhere. What does that suggest to you?"

"A gypsy tearoom."

"I've always wondered," she said, "why psychologists play this game, and now I know. Now—what suggests itself to your freely associating mind as a next step?"

"Good God, Natalie," he exploded, "do you know how many gypsy tearooms there are in this town?"

"No. Do you?"

"Damn near two hundred, if you count every joint that has a fortune teller. And that's not counting astrologers and mediums."

"All fortune tellers aren't astrologers," Natalie pointed out, "nor are all astrologers fortune tellers."

"Maybe," Harrison suggested with a straight face, "I should make tea, so's you can read the leaves."

"All right," Jensen snapped, "knock it off! If you've got bright ideas, how about suggesting a place to start?"

"The Spanish quarter," Natalie said firmly.

Jensen nodded and reached for his notebook. "Whoever said women aren't logical should be shot. Who's in charge downtown, Turk?"

"Joe Myers."

"I'm going to call him," Jensen said, "and see how much help we can have. You lend Natalie some moral support coming down those stairs. She may need it."

"You getting a warrant?" Harrison asked.

"On what grounds?" Jensen countered. "No judge in his right mind would issue one on this combination of suspicion, circumstantial evidence, and outright imagination. No—if we find Duval, we'll have to improvise and take her in for spitting on the sidewalk or something."

"What about Peter Archer?" Natalie asked suddenly.

Jensen paused in the doorway. "He'll be released right after breakfast. After all, we can't turn him out hungry, can we?"

By the time Harrison and Natalie, who was grateful for his assistance, got downstairs, Jensen was deep in conversation with his superior. While they waited, Natalie found a pair of sunglasses and put then on to hide her battered eye. Jensen came in while she was repairing her hairdo and teased her mildly about being incognito.

"We have a psychology instructor," she commented, "an earnest youth, who maintains that only paranoids wear sunglasses indoors. I look forward to giving him some embarrassing moments in the next few days. Are we off and running, Chris?"

He nodded. "Are you sure you want to stick this out, or shall we deliver you to Professor Ken?"

"I'll stick," she said.

"If we find her," he warned, "it won't be pleasant. It may be—it won't be very pretty."

"Is anything wrong, Chris?"

"I hope not." He sounded distracted. "Let's go—"

CHAPTER XIV

"I don't know what you propose doing at this hour," Natalie said, settling herself on the front seat between the two detectives, "but I assume you have something in mind."

"Optimist!" Harrison said.

Jensen laughed soundlessly. "I've got an idea, but it's still too vague to be called a plan."

"I wouldn't object if you told me about it," Natalie said.

"Neither would I," Harrison added, slowing for a light.

"Well, if you'll both shut up, I will!"

"Okay"—Harrison grinned—"okay, okay."

"Most police forces," Jensen began after a pause, "and we're no exception, maintain special squads to keep track of known swindlers, racketeers, bad-check artists, and the like. They also keep lists of spiritualists, mediums, and their ilk. Step the first in our battle plan is to check these lists for likely prospects."

"What's step number two?" Natalie asked.

"Don't ask embarrassing questions, Professor," Harrison cautioned.

She giggled. "I know exactly how he feels."

She sensed rather than saw Jensen's smile, and settled herself more comfortably in the reassuring company of these two men. A week ago, she reflected, they had been strangers and threatening; ten days ago, she had not even known they existed. Now, in a frighteningly real sense, she owed them her life. Yet what she felt was not just obligation: it was the friendship of one human being for others, a willingness to trust and a gratitude for being trusted.

She considered these two, whom once she would have considered it beneath her to know and to like. Just as the war had created friendships as lasting as they were sometimes ill assorted, so this smaller, more personal agony was binding its survivors uniquely together. On the face of it, it was a contradiction in terms to seek good in the aftermath of an event as raw and horrible as murder, yet it was there. Like the brilliant and graceful fireweed that thrives best where the earth has been seared by flame, the astonishing human capacity for good seemed always most active in the wake of evil.

It made her feel old to recall her small part in a war that had ended while some of her students were still in their playpens. But in a way she felt younger for reviving the idealism that had wilted in the safe aridity of her postwar life. The past is never so immediate as in one's own present.

I'm changing, she thought; and I don't think it's just "foxhole religion" either. It's as if, in dying, Will has given me one last gift. He always cared so deeply for people, and I never could—until now.

The night had reached its intermediate stage when neither light nor darkness stood dominant. For Natalie Keith the lesser measurements of time, the minutes and hours, had long ago ceased to have meaning. It was only in this, the greater shift, the alternation of night and day, that mattered. Darkness and light—life and death: perhaps, after all, the world was just that simple.

"Hey," Turk Harrison said suddenly, "there's Jerry Gant on the corner!"

"Probably waiting for a ride." Jensen rolled down his window.

Harrison brought the car to the curb and stopped.

"Want a lift, buddy?" Jensen called.

Detective Gant, looking more like a truck driver than a policeman, flipped his cigarette into the gutter and trotted over. "Wouldn't mind. Going as far as Market Street?"

"Market and Purchase," Jensen answered amiably. "Climb in back."

"What's the matter," Harrison asked, "cab drivers all wise to your 'no-tip' motto?"

"Sure looks that way," Gant replied. "What's with you?"

"A lot and nothing," Jensen told him. "Natalie, meet Detective Jerome Gant, who taught me all I know about this business. Jerry—Doctor Natalie Keith."

"Pleased to meet you." Gant reached over the seat to shake hands.

"May I have a rain check?" Natalie asked with a wry grin, holding up her bandaged left hand. "I'm at a social disadvantage."

"Geez," Gant marveled, "what've these two been doing to you?"

"I lost an argument with a truck," she answered cockily.

"The Santos business," Jensen explained, "it's all part of the Gregg case."

"That's a dog, that one," Gant said wisely. "You getting anywhere, Chris?"

"We could be getting everywhere," he answered wistfully, "all we need is the right fortune teller."

Gant considered in silence. "Is it *that* bad?"

Harrison offered an astonishingly canine growl in answer, and Jensen went on to explain. Listening to the unfamiliar jargon of the trade, Natalie experienced the first twinge of separation from this thing that had occupied the whole of her being for seven days. In sparse, technical terms, the murder of Will Gregg and the search for his killer became an episode of which she, an associate professor of History, could not possibly have been a part.

"You don't have a picture of this dame, do you?" Gant asked casually.

"No," Jensen said, "why?"

"Day before yesterday," he answered, "I got word of a new medium operating on my beat. Your description—if you could call it that—seems to fit. I've got the address if you want it."

Harrison pulled to the curb and stopped. "Go?" he asked.

"Go!" Jensen answered and turned to Natalie. "You realize that this isn't really happening. It's absolutely impossible for three people to whip up a paperback plot like this and have it work out."

"I've had a brain concussion—what's your excuse?"

Jerry Gant laughed, and she knew that he had accepted her

178

as part of the machine that he, quite by chance and with better credentials, had just joined. Another policeman who had become a friend.

Turk Harrison, driving with the casual skill of one whose knowledge of a city is more reflex than conscious, brought them quickly into the Spanish section. Once it had been the Italian section; before then, it had been the Irish section. It was indeed a section where roots were put down. There were many who would have liked to forget it, but for the student of humanity it was vital and fascinating. In the nascent day, Natalie recognized it as Babylon, Thebes, Knossos, Byblos, Ostia— the modern incarnation of every city that has ever forced the confrontation of men of differing race and tongue; the eternal human experiment with humanity.

"That's it, by the Greek restaurant." Gant pointed to a two-story brick house with scrubbed white steps and lace curtains.

"How well do you know the landlady?" Jensen asked.

"How well does a man know his mother?" Gant asked. "That well I know Mrs. Ramos. But never from trouble, Chris, never. Her husband drank himself to death, and she raised two sons who turned out good, and a daughter who's a nun."

"Has she ever had trouble with a boarder before?"

"Once or twice. That's how we met. Usually if she isn't sure, she calls me, like she did with this one."

Jensen rolled up his window and put his right hand on the door handle. "We'd better go in. You carry it, Jerry, and I'll follow. Natalie, you stick close to Turk."

"Don't look now"—Harrison opened his door and stepped out into the street—"but someone's watching from the top right corner window."

"I noticed," Jensen said, leading the way toward the front door. "Does Mrs. Ramos have both floors, Jerry?"

"Yeah." He rang the bell. "That was probably her watching."

Natalie, suddenly afraid, wished they would give her a night stick or something to hold on to. Then the front door opened on a chain, and she saw a small, stout woman in a dark robe peering out.

179

"I'm sorry to be so late, *Mamacita*," Gant began softly, "but I'd like to talk to you."

"Ah, Jerry!" she said, "a moment—a moment—" She closed the door and the chain dropped. "Come in, please."

Gant made the introductions in rapid, if oddly accented, Spanish, always deferring to Jensen yet remaining clearly the spokesman. Mrs. Ramos, not at all disturbed by the invasion of police, settled them in her worn but pleasant living room and did her best to answer their questions.

"What you wish is the informations, no?" she asked.

Gant nodded, "That's right, Mamma. There's a woman calling herself Juanita Valdez. Is she here?"

"*Ay, Madre de Dios!*" Mrs. Ramos crossed herself. "I was going to call you again in the morning. She is evil, that one. Three nights she has been here, and already I am afraid."

"How do you mean, 'evil,' Señora?" Jensen asked.

"To bother the dead, *Teniente*," the old woman answered gravely, "this is evil. It is to spit in the face of God."

"Is that what she does, Señora?" Jensen pressed gently. "Does she call the dead to speak to the living?"

"*Sí.*" The old woman sounded relieved that it was he who said the words. "This very night, here in my parlor, she tempted others with her own sin."

Gant and Jensen looked at each other. "Jerry will go with you, Señora," Jensen told her, "while you wake this woman. Tell her there are people in the parlor who have heard of her powers and wish a séance."

"I think," Natalie said suddenly, "that it's too late to hold a séance."

"Probably," Jensen agreed, "but Jerry'll think of something."

They were silent; she sitting in an armchair in the corner behind the opened door, while Harrison waited on the other side and Jensen stood in the center of the room.

"They're coming," he said finally, watching through the doorway. "What a night this has turned out to be!"

"I am Juanita Valdez," a voice announced, "descendant of the priests of Quetzalcoatl, the Shining Serpent. What do you wish of me?"

180

She came into the room and stopped short when she saw Jensen. Natalie, from her semi-concealment, could see clearly a woman in an austere black dress with her dark hair pulled back to accentuate the severe angularity of her features.

Like a nun, Natalie thought; like a nun consecrated to an antichrist.

"It is too late," the woman said, "I cannot hold another séance tonight. Come back tomorrow."

Jensen shook his head. "We have questions that cannot wait. Come and sit down, Miss Duval."

With one quick movement, Renata Duval turned first to her right, saw Turk Harrison standing by the wall, and then to her left, where Natalie sat, partially hidden.

"Who are you?" she demanded.

"You know us," Jensen said. "We met a week ago, at the home of Professor Gregg—the late Professor Gregg."

"I dislike your bad jokes, young man. In Mexico City I would not be treated in this way. They respect the blood of Aztec kings that is in my veins."

"Your name," Jensen told her, "is Renata Duval. Until last week, you were employed by Doctor Wilson Gregg as his secretary."

"You dare!— Who are you?"

"Police." Jensen showed her his shield. "Christopher Jensen, Lieutenant, Homicide. Come and sit here at the table."

The strange woman in the center of the circle hesitated, then nodded and obeyed. "I understand. Homicide has to do with death, and you seek my help. But I cannot help you. It is too late."

"I think you can," Jensen said. "Mrs. Keith, if you will—"

Natalie got up and came forward, never once taking her eyes from this woman who was both known and a stranger to her.

"Mrs. Keith, have you ever met this person before?"

"Yes, Lieutenant, I have. Only I know her as Renata Duval, secretary to the late Doctor Gregg."

"She lies! I am Valdez, priestess of Quetzalcoatl. You are persecuting me!"

It occurred to Natalie with leaden coldness that perhaps she did not remember last week, or the part of her life she had lived in it. She stared for a moment into the curiously bright and curiously flat eyes of this bewildering woman, and then shook her head.

"No, Renata," she said, "it won't do. Your right ear is pierced twice because you had poison ivy two years ago that got infected and sealed the original hole. Will's doctor took care of you."

The woman rose and flung herself toward Natalie, hands stretched out and clutching for her throat. Jensen and Harrison moved simultaneously to catch her, deftly thwarting the attack and returning her to the chair. Natalie, stupefied, stood unmoving.

"Witch!" Duval screamed. "You are a witch!"

Jensen's hand closed over her mouth and her belligerence guttered out.

"What do you want?" she asked sullenly.

"Where have you been for the past seven days?" Jensen asked.

"At the home of my ancestors."

"We know," he began in a gentle tone that would wear like an abrasive on human resistance, "that you did not board the two-thirty plane to New Orleans last week. We know that you did not visit the Marvin Endicot family in New Orleans because there is no such family. Where were you, Miss Duval?"

She said nothing, and he began again. "After you left Doctor Gregg's house at noon last Wednesday, you came back to get some papers and his bronze hawk. Where did you go after that? And again that afternoon, after four, where did you go? When you came back after nine-fifteen that night, did you see Peter Archer leaving?— We know you came back, Mrs. Duval."

"I am not married."

"Then why don't you use the name Hernandes?"

"I know no one by that name."

"You entered the United States in Texas, I believe. I have the dates and the name of the immigration officer in charge. It will be easy enough to verify. And then there's Carla Duval—"

"Carla is my niece."

"Then you no longer claim to be Juanita Valdez—"

She looked at him, and for a moment Natalie pitied her. "What are you doing to me?" she wailed.

"I'm trying to understand you."

"You can't! How could you?"

"At the moment," Jensen admitted, "you're right. I do not and cannot understand you. But I intend to try, Mrs. Duval, because I'm very concerned about Carla."

Renata Duval twisted toward him with an almost feline yowl of challenge. "Go out into the street," she shouted, "get a woman of your own sort! But leave Carla alone—do you hear?—leave her alone, you son of a skinny pig!"

Jensen raised his voice just enough to force her attention. "You are, I presume, the next of kin."

Renata Duval's face, livid with anger one moment, was closed and suspicious the next. "Why?"

"Carla Duval died an hour ago, at Urban Hospital, of a brain injury."

The intense, distrustful face went slowly blank, and Renata Duval slumped in her seat. Jensen caught her and steadied her while Harrison crushed a glass ampule and held it under her nose. She responded slowly, and sat staring at her hands.

"Tell me about it," Jensen urged gently.

"My daughter, she's my daughter. But she never knew it. I had her raised in a convent, and when I sent for her I told her I was her aunt and that her mother was dead. Her father—he—we never had the priest. When I found a baby was coming he vanished."

"How long did you work for Doctor Gregg?"

"Five years." Renata Duval straightened and ran both hands across her forehead and back over her hair. "He was a good man, and kind. I wanted to make a decent home for Carla, and I wrote to Will that I needed a job. He never knew about Carla, except that she was my niece."

"That took a lot of courage, Mrs. Duval," Jensen said.

She looked to him, and for one moment Natalie saw reason and calmness in her eyes.

"How was she killed?" she asked.

"Do you know a man called Dave Santos? Or maybe you knew him as Ramón Santiago—"

"Yes. He is a Cuban who works for the FBI, investigating Castro agents in this country, so he calls himself Santiago. He's in love with Carla and wants to marry her. Really marry her, I mean. In a church."

"Dave Santos killed Carla, Mrs. Duval," Jensen told her. "Mrs. Keith was a witness."

"Where is he now?"

"I killed him," Natalie said before she could stop herself.

Renata Duval turned to her, and Natalie forgot that there was anyone else in the room. There existed between this turbulent woman and herself a momentary bond as strong as it was elusive.

"Then there is blood on both our hands," Renata Duval said, "and I am your debtor."

"How did it happen, Renata? About Will, I mean—"

"Dave told you about that?" she asked bitterly, "I thought Dave would marry my Carla, but I had no money for a wedding. I asked Will Gregg for a thousand dollars, but he said the best he could manage was five hundred. It wasn't enough for a wedding and a dowry, and I told him so. He said it was the best he could do and that he was sorry, and all I could think was that without a dowry Dave would do to Carla what her father had done to me, and I got angry and I picked something up and hit him with it until he fell over. I knew I had killed him, and there was that thing, that god-bird sitting on his desk that had seen me do it so I took it with me and I ran. I ran as fast and as far as I could, and Dave said I mustn't keep the god-bird so I left it home. You understand how it was, don't you?"

Natalie nodded. "Did Dave know you had hurt Will?"

"Yes. And when the policeman called he said I must go and tell them everything except that I had hit Will. He gave me the name of some people in New Orleans for me to say I had to visit because one of them was my sister. I wonder why he did that? I don't know anyone in New Orleans any more. And he was there—Dave, I mean—at the airport when the policeman drove me out there, and he took me away and told me to hide until Monday and then to come here because I am a priestess of Quetzalcoatl and have the power to speak to those who have gone."

She's insane, Natalie thought; or else she's the world's greatest actress. But I can't hate her—somehow I can't hate her.

"Renata Maria Alicia Hernandes Duval," Jensen said, sounding suddenly tired and discouraged, "do you know what I am?"

"A policeman," she answered.

"Yes, a policeman, and I must arrest you for the murder of Wilson Gregg."

"I didn't mean to—"

"I understand, and I'm sure Mrs. Keith does. But I have to arrest you and take you to a judge. Perhaps he will understand too."

Renata Duval looked at him and smiled with the terrible simplicity of those who are beyond understanding. "It is the stars that ordain what we must do. You say you must arrest me, and so it must be that the stars have determined it. What is your birth date? I must know that to cast a horoscope. Oh, and your name. What is your given name?"

"Christopher."

"Ah—that means 'Christ-bearer,' you know." She broke off and her face puckered with sudden emotion. "My daughter is dead, you know. I want her to have a real funeral, with a real priest."

"She will," Jensen said, "I promise."

"May I go to it?"

"Yes."

She's a child, Natalie thought; a vicious, conscienceless child with no more real emotion than a snake, but still a child.

"Are you going to take me to prison now?"

"Yes," Jensen told her, "but not in my car. My sergeant will call for a special car."

"You are a gentleman." Renata Duval bowed toward him. "I shall see that They know about you."

It was a gesture of dismissal, and Natalie was aware that Jensen too accepted it as such. He nodded to Jerry Gant, who stepped forward to take charge, and then took Natalie's arm

185

and steered her gently toward the door. Turk Harrison and Mrs. Ramos followed.

"I'm afraid I'll have to ask for another statement, Natalie," he said, "but it'll be the last, I promise."

She nodded and sat in the nearest chair. "It's all over, isn't it, Chris?"

"Almost. Soon it'll be up to twelve other people and the law."

"An imperfect instrument in unskilled hands," she said, suddenly weary with the weight of irony inherent in her own words, "this whole thing—it has such a—a fated quality to it, as if we were all playing parts. I wish some people who've laughed at Renata could have seen what happened in there."

"I know," he said inadequately.

"I think Will understood her, somehow. I can forgive her, if he could."

"Can you?"

"I don't know. I don't know if my forgiveness would make any difference. I'm a murderer too."

Impulsively, he reached out and put his hand on her shoulder. She relaxed under his touch and leaned back in the chair.

"I'm tired," she admitted, "bone tired."

"It's almost over."

"I keep thinking about poor, lost little Carla. Killing her was so unnecessary."

Turk Harrison came back and reported that an ambulance with a policewoman aboard was on the way to take Renata Duval to Urban Hospital for observation. He added that the captain was pleased.

"Pleased, hell!" Jensen said bitterly. "Take over, Turk. I'm going to take Natalie to Doctor Ken's house so she can rest."

CHAPTER XV

Not until Jensen had driven several blocks from Mrs. Ramos's rooming house did Natalie feel able to speak again. Even then, her voice was unsteady.

"What happened to Carla?" she asked.

Jensen hesitated and shifted his grip on the wheel. "According to the doctor, a neurosurgeon named McIvor or McIntyre or something, she probably had a weak spot in one of the arteries of the brain that burst when she was hit. An aneurysm, he called it. Anyhow, she went into a coma and didn't respond to treatment. They did all they could, but it wasn't enough."

"In a way, I guess it's merciful. She'd have been cut to pieces by the things that'll come out at Renata's trial."

"Actually, Nat, I doubt that she'll come to trial. I'm pretty sure she'll be committed."

"Then you think she's insane—"

"It's not mine to say. I'm neither a psychiatrist nor a judge. I'm just a cop."

"But if she's not—if she's acting. To spend the rest of her life in a mental hospital—"

"The law isn't proof against irony."

His words hung a long time in the forefront of her thoughts. Was it the law, or justice or life itself, that shaped and imposed what many chose to call irony? Or was it a trick of the human mind, measuring the events of life against an inward vision of what ought to be?

"There are a couple of knots left to untie, Natalie," Jensen said. "Shall I take you to Doctor Ken's now, or could you survive another visit to the Duval apartment?"

"I'm like Sir Gawain in the Mabinogion Cycle. My strength waxeth until the noontide."

"Whereafter, I presume, it waneth. This won't take long, I promise."

Natalie smiled but said nothing until Jensen found a parking place and eased the car into it.

"You know," she sighed, "it's funny—I still can't fix this place on my mental map. Do you suppose I need a psychiatrist?"

"Eh-eh. Just a night's sleep."

"Fine pair we are," she agreed with a straight face, "you're beat down, and I'm beat up!"

Inside, Jensen produced a passkey to the Duval apartment. "Turk had trouble getting this," he remarked, "the manager wanted to know how long it would be before he could advertise for new tenants."

Natalie shuddered. "I can't imagine wanting to live in the apartment of a murderer, can you?"

"No, but ours is an age vastly amused by the morbid. Will it bother you to wait inside?"

She shook her head. "Go earn your salary. I'll be in the living room—if you could call it that."

She walked away from him, wondering at her own lack of emotion. On a chair near the door, much nearer than she remembered, lay the bronze Horus, its blue-green patina showing well against the umber-colored upholstery.

She leaned down and tried to pick up the Horus, but the tortured muscles of her left hand refused the weight. Instead, she sat and eased it into her lap. For an instant, the inlaid eyes seemed alive and knowing.

Jensen began to whistle as he searched, and she remembered that Ben Keith had had the same habit. She had always known his mood by what he whistled: show tunes for boredom, jazz for frustration, Bach or Beethoven for moments of discovery, and Mozart for triumph. She had once seen him flat on his stomach, clearing dirt from fragments of a Mycenaean fresco with a paintbrush, and performing whole sections of the Jupiter Symphony.

You, she thought, glowering at the Horus, wouldn't rate a fast chorus of "Pop Goes the Weasel." Only when I found you,

I got so excited— God, if I'd known, I'd have thrown you into the Nile!

Jensen leaned into the room. "Natalie? You okay?"

"I guess so. Did you find what you need?"

"Nope. Is that the famous bronze bird?"

"Yes. I was just wishing I'd never found him."

"You're positive you did—"

"Here are my numbers. I presume Sir Hugh still has the dig records if you want to check."

"I don't, but the district attorney probably will. Who'd you say this fella represents?"

"Whom," she corrected, and he grinned at her, "he's Horus, a prehistoric Egyptian sun-god who was grafted into the later mythology as the son of Isis and Osiris, and who avenged the murder of his father. In fact," she added, a sudden chill striking through her, "he's the nearest thing to a god of vengeance the Egyptians ever had."

Jensen, his face grave and his eyes thoughtful, was silent a moment before answering. "Near enough, near enough."

"Chris"—Natalie ran her free hand over the rhythmic curves of the hawk's back—"what're you going to do with me?"

"Oh," he answered, "feed you breakfast, I guess, and then deliver you to Doctor Ken. Why?"

"That's not exactly what I meant. I've killed a man, after all—"

He came and stood in front of her, a young man suddenly become her teacher. "The law has no claim against you, Natalie," he told her, "nor should you have one against yourself. What you did was done to save your own life and to help the law, not hinder it. I know it's a terrible feeling— God, how well I know it!—but there's nothing criminal about it."

"Not by the letter of the law, perhaps."

"Nor by the spirit. You didn't act in malice, or in the spirit of revenge."

She said nothing, but looked past him at the gold-colored rug where the outline of a body had been marked in blue chalk. "There's that too," she said, "Carla—"

"That's on Dave Santos's soul, not yours."

189

"Of course," she said with surprising bitterness, "the innocent bystander—"

"So was Doctor Gregg," Jensen reminded her. "The world is full of innocent bystanders who get hurt. Evil is a very real force in human affairs, and you don't have to be religious to be aware of it. It has a high velocity. You're no more to blame for what's happened than is Doctor Gregg."

She turned sharply and looked at him.

"I've shocked you, because I intended to. But you could blame *him* for this, you know. After all, he had no obligation, moral or otherwise, to get involved with Renata Hernandes-Duval."

"*He* thought he did."

"Sure, because he was a good man. You know, I sometimes think that the good people in this world are responsible for most of the evil. They make it so easy for the twisted and greedy."

"And just where," Natalie demanded with difficulty, "did you get that idea?"

He shrugged. "It evolved. But as I see it—and I admit to being a heretic in every sense of the word—either we're all responsible for each other, or we're all totally irresponsible."

Natalie was aware of the passage of her fingers over the time-roughened bronze of the Horus. "Not heretical," she said slowly, "not even particularly unconventional. Just rather too blunt for most of us to bear."

He said nothing, but reached down and took the Horus from her. "I'll have to keep this for a while, but you'll get him back. I'll even give you a receipt."

With the last of her strength, she responded to his change of subject with an adroit shift of mood. "Have it notarized," she said, "or I won't accept it."

"I'll seal it with the print of my right great toe," he answered, grinning, "now come on—I'm taking you to Doctor Ken."

She did not protest, but got up meekly and went with him.

It was an in-and-out morning, with the early sun barely able to assert itself between gray clouds. The city, long awake and stirring, seemed at this time to have paused before plunging fully

190

into the depths of the day's work. As Jensen drove, Natalie watched men and women leaving their homes, saw others straggling into cars or standing dazedly at bus stops, waiting. Another day of history being written in terms of flesh and blood and work. Had it ever, she wondered, been any other way?

Edward Ken came out of his house and started down the walk as Jensen parked. Natalie wanted to wave, but the effort seemed too great and she sat still and watched him come.

"I was hoping you'd come before I left." Ken opened the door for her. "Come in, both of you. Michi's just starting breakfast."

"Thanks," Jensen said, "and forgive me if I don't join you. The day's just starting for me."

"I can imagine." Ken nodded. "All the donkey work still to be done. Tell me, did you find Renata?"

Jensen nodded, and the three of them started up the path with Natalie in the middle. "We found her," he answered, "end of Act One. . . . Natalie, take care, and remember the things I've said."

"I'll try," she promised, "when this is all over, and I can wriggle my fingers again, I want you and Laura and Turk to come for dinner."

He smiled and then, on impulse, leaned down and kissed her on the cheek. "We'll be there, Nat, with bells on. So long for now, and take care!"

He turned and went, and Natalie leaned slightly against Edward Ken as her knees went weak. He put his arm around her and started slowly back up the front steps.

"Steady does it, old girl."

"It's been a long night, and I'm cold."

"It's brisk," he agreed, "but a good cup of Irish coffee'll help. And after that, Professor, you are going to sleep the clock around."

Natalie was silent, grateful that he seemed uninterested in the night's doings or her part in them. Tomorrow she would tell him about it. Tomorrow—not today.

Jensen tooted his horn jauntily as he drove away, and Natalie turned to wave him on his way. She watched as he merged

with the other traffic, and stood a moment longer just considering the day and the fact that she was alive to know it.

"All right, Natalie?"

"Yes," she said, believing her own words, "I'm all right,
thanks to my friends."

Osiris died in autumn, and after Isis had buried his scattered
parts the life-giving wheat had sprouted from his grave. Will
Gregg had also died in autumn, and as she stood in the sun
and shadow of a day she had almost missed beholding, Natalie
Keith realized that she too had a legacy awaiting harvest: never
again would she be able to live uncaring for the rest of humankind.

F: